KILLER FLOWERS

A CHRISTIE'S FLOWER SHOPPE COZY MYSTERY

PJ PETERSON

Copyright © 2023 by PJ Peterson

All rights reserved.

No part of this book may be reproduced in any form or by any electronic or mechanical means, including information storage and retrieval systems, without written permission from the author, except for the use of brief quotations in a book review.

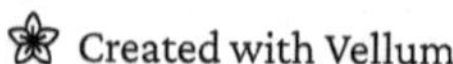 Created with Vellum

DEDICATION

This book is dedicated to all the talented individuals who take the challenge to open and operate their own businesses.
It takes courage, time, and a lot of determination to be a success. It's more difficult than working forty hours a week for someone else and I admire those who are willing to become those independent entrepreneurs. Small businesses are the backbone of America's business world.
My own mother had a small handcrafts business here in my hometown. She delighted in teaching others how to create beautiful things with their hands. When I was a kid, she frequently taught classes of all kinds at Girl Scout meetings, and made life-like fiber flowers for weddings and other events. Even my dad got into the act and learned how to do macramé and glass etching.
Hats off, America!

CHAPTER
ONE

The wind howled outside on Friday afternoon in late October, and the lights flickered off for a moment while Christie O'Mara floated around the flower and gift shop. She flicked an imaginary wisp of dust off an antique cherry writing desk. She straightened a ribbon bow on the gigantic vase of fresh flowers sitting on the glass table next to her order station. A bouquet of balloons danced in front of the fan that she had placed strategically behind the display.

Christie clasped her hands together and smiled at the transformation before her eyes. She was ready for the grand re-opening the next day of the florist shop which had belonged to her grandma. Because it was the week before Halloween, she had decorated with a ghostly theme using witches and pumpkins against a purple and orange backdrop.

Six weeks ago, her mother had called with the sad news that Grandma Maude O'Mara had died unexpectedly. Christie recalled the many happy hours she had spent helping her grandma and Aunt Doris in the shop, and she grieved the loss of this special person in her life. She was thankful that she had been able to have a long conversation with her a week before her death, not knowing it would be the last.

Christie had spent weekends and summers at the shop. She had been fascinated to learn both the flowers' names and their meanings. Her aunt, who was actually her great-aunt, her grandfather's younger sister, had patiently taught Christie how to arrange flowers in beautiful bouquets and displays. One summer, Christie took a class in the Japanese art of ikebana, and reveled in the simple yet elegant designs she learned to create.

But as a teenager, she had dreamed of living in a big, exciting city and being on her own with a brilliant future in business ahead of her. So, she'd headed out of her small home-town to college and earned a degree in business with a minor in accounting. However, the reality of her job and the big city was something totally different from her fantasy.

She had been passed over a couple of times for a higher-level position, possibly due to her refusal to get "better acquainted" with her male boss. An attempt to file a sexual harassment suit at her work was strongly discouraged by the company's head of Human Resources — another male. She had been seriously looking for a position in a new company when she learned of her grandmother's death.

WHEN HER MOTHER called a few weeks later to inform her that if she didn't want to take over the shop, it would be sold or closed, all those fond memories of their times together in that shop flooded back yet again — but this time with joy. Christie made the decision to leave her job and San Francisco and become a florist shop owner instead. The very next day, she turned in her notice at the furniture store chain where she worked as the lead accountant.

And now Christie was back in her hometown of White Castle. She looked forward to being her own boss and making her own mark in the world. And there would be no one in her way holding her back. She would have the help of her Aunt Doris, who had been her grandma's right-hand "man" for years and who was thrilled that Christie would continue the business. Sometimes, Christie thought her aunt was a little goofy, but she certainly knew the language of flowers and was bound to be helpful for continuity with the community when her grandma's longtime customers came through the door.

Christie would continue the basics of making and selling floral bouquets, of course, but she also planned to expand the gifts section that she thought could use some freshening up. When she surveyed the space, she was intrigued to find a dozen or so pieces of vintage and antique furniture begging to be polished up and displayed. They had been stored in a large closet in the back of the shop. Aunt Doris had told her that Grandma Maude hadn't gotten around to doing anything with them, although she'd talked about selling the items as another means of bringing in customers and money. It felt good to know she was completing a plan her grandma had not gotten around to fulfilling.

During the previous week, Christie and her mother had spent several afternoons cleaning up the dainty desks, small tables, and even a tall, freestanding vintage radio. Her mom explained that she had listened to radio shows on it as a child when she visited her own grandparents. She had been enthralled to listen to the stories being told over the air while drinking hot chocolate and eating homemade cookies.

On the eve of the grand reopening, one last piece remained to be readied for sale: the writing desk. It was a lovely piece, and she felt almost sad that she had decided to sell it, but she didn't have any emotional attachment to it and hoped someone would love it enough to pay its price. She stood next to it with her arms crossed for a moment and took a big breath before doing a final inspection.

She checked to be sure the legs were secure, polished the entire piece, and pulled out each of the drawers one at a time. She shook out the dust and other bits that had collected over the years of use or disuse. When she inverted the last one, the bottom drawer on the right, she found an envelope taped to the underside.

Curious, Christie loosened the yellowed tape and carefully lifted the envelope from the drawer's wooden surface. The envelope read "Missy." There was no street address. She guessed it must have been given to Missy in person instead of being mailed. The glue had long since dried, so the flap opened readily. She gently removed from the envelope the single piece of fragile stationery embossed with the letter 'M' that had been folded in half, and opened it. She read:

My dear Missy,

I HOPE you will understand that circumstances have arisen that cause me to leave town immediately. I do not know when I can return or if I will ever be able to see you again.

I HOPE you will ignore any rumors that I killed anyone. I swear it wasn't me. There were a bunch of guys involved in the fight, but I didn't know any of them. Maybe the sheriff will figure out the truth.

B.

. . .

SHE ASKED HERSELF ALOUD, "Who are Missy and B? And who died? I wonder if Aunt Doris would know." She folded the letter and put it back in the envelope, then placed it in the drawer of her work desk. "Maybe she'll remember how Grandma Maude got this desk, and then we could figure out who Missy was."

CHRISTIE TOOK one last look around the shop and sighed happily. She picked up her tote bag, an umbrella and the shop keys and went out the back door. As she stepped out, she almost tripped over a black lump in the middle of the single step. "Meow," the black lump cried as it stood up, arching its back.

"A kitty! A *black* kitty," Christie exclaimed, grinning at the thought of discovering it so close to Halloween. Without any superstitious inclinations, she bent over to get a closer look. "You're all wet." She picked up the small cat and went back inside, where she found a towel and dried it off. The kitty started purring and licked Christie's chin. "I wonder if Grandma had been feeding you, and that's why you're hanging out here. Let's check for cat food in the closet." Christie checked the cabinet in the bathroom and, sure enough, found a partial bag of cat kibble, confirming her suspicion. She grabbed a couple of plastic flowerpot saucers from the supply cupboard to serve as dishes for food and water.

Christie stood with her hands on her hips and watched as the cat ate hungrily. She would check around to see if it belonged to someone nearby, but by the way it scarfed down the food, she doubted it had a home. She recalled a favorite mystery series in which a bookstore owner had a cat named Agatha in honor of Agatha Christie. "Hmm. Would you like to be my shop cat? I would expect you to be polite to the customers and clean up after yourself. Of course, that is unless someone else claims you." She made a mental note to drop by the grocery store in the next block and pick up a litter box and kitty litter. She figured she would be spending more hours at the store than at her home for the first few weeks anyway, and the cat would provide company while she was there.

Her cell phone buzzed in the tote bag sitting on the counter. Aunt Doris's name popped up. "Hi, Aunt Doris. Hey. Did Grandma feed a black kitty at the shop?"

"Did that scrawny thing show up again? I kept shooing it away, but I know she was sneaking food to it when she didn't think I would notice."

Christie chuckled. That sounded like something her grandma would have done. "Yes, it's probably the same kitty. I thought I would let it be a mascot for the shop. You wouldn't mind, would you?"

Aunt Doris snorted. "You're just like your grandmother, you know. She had the softest heart." Her voice softened. "I don't mind. It'll keep us company when business is slow. I suppose you've named it already."

"Not yet, but 'Stormy' comes to mind, seeing as it's a black cat and it's 'a dark and stormy night' outside. I hope Charles Schulz would agree that she fits that line from his *Peanuts* cartoons."

"That's a good name, honey. Are you ready for the big day tomorrow? I saw the event posted on Facebook, and there was a copy of the newspaper notice posted at the pharmacy."

"As ready as I'm going to be. I thought I'd come over about eight thirty. Can you be here that early?"

"Sure. I'll bring a coffee urn," replied her aunt. "I've ordered pastries and frosted cookies that say 'Christie's' from the bakery to be delivered when we open. I thought we could have them at the front table where customers sign up for email. I kept telling Maude that she should get modern and do that."

"Good idea, Auntie. An email list is important these days, even for a small business like the flower shop. I've saved a space on the table for the coffee and goodies."

"Are you going to leave that cat at the shop alone tonight?"

"I thought I would take the kitty home with me and pick up cat stuff on the way there." The cat snuggled and purred loudly in Christie's arms. "I think Stormy likes that idea. She's already adopted me. See you in the morning."

"Will do. I'll keep my fingers crossed that everything goes well for you tomorrow."

Christie smiled as the call ended. Crossed fingers weren't her way of handling things. She liked good planning and logical approaches. "I don't think crossed fingers bring good fortune any more than a black cat crossing my path means bad luck. Right, Stormy?"

CHAPTER

TWO

By one o'clock, it seemed as if half of the small town's population had come through the doors of the floral shop, rechristened as Christie's Flower Shoppe. The town's mayor, who had been a classmate of her father, came by with a proclamation declaring the occasion as "Christie's Flower Shoppe Day." He also reminded her to vote in the upcoming election. *Always the politician*, Christie thought to herself.

Aunt Doris kept busy at the main counter selling gifts, cards and ready-made bouquets, as well as taking orders for delivery items for the next week. The email signup list had fifty names on it by noon, much to Christie's delight. Stormy perched herself on the top of a cabinet from whence she held reign over the shop next to a framed picture of a street with a sign that read "Flower Power." Christie wondered if the sign had originally come from the Haight-Ashbury district of San Francisco, perhaps taken by Aunt Doris herself.

One of the surprises of the day was seeing her high school friend, Anita Sanders, stroll into the shop. She had moved into

White Castle from Seattle as a high school freshman and initially struggled to make friends. The girls in her class were jealous because all the boys promptly vied for her attention. She slowly and quietly adapted to the politics of a small high school and became part of the fabric. She and Christie had shared a love of volleyball and became friends on the school team. Though they'd been good buddies through high school, they hadn't kept in touch during the final year of college and their early adulthood. Anita, with her family money, had gone the sorority route at Stanford while Christie had worked her way through college at the state university, usually holding down two jobs at a time to supplement her scholarship support.

Christie, with a mop of golden curls and a strong, athletic body, had been more inclined to play pickup games of soccer and softball in college, while Anita attended plays and musicals with her sorority pals. In retrospect, it was a surprise in a way that they had been such good friends at all, but such was the way in smaller communities where proximity was the primary driver.

At thirty-two, Anita was still tall and lean, with an aristocratic face and blue eyes framed by her long, dark hair. Christie had sparkly Irish green eyes and hints of red in her golden hair, courtesy of the O'Mara genes, that fit her bubbly personality.

"Anita! What a surprise to see you!" Christie excused herself from a conversation and went to give her old friend a hug. "Are you visiting family?"

Anita shook her head and hugged Christie, then stepped back and put her hands on Christie's shoulders. "You look just the same as you did in high school. I'm surprised to see you in your grandma's shop. What happened to the big city life you used to talk about?"

Christy shrugged. "Tried it. Didn't like it as much as I

thought I would. So here I am back home, taking a breather while I revisit my future."

"Sounds like me. A degree in anthropology with a minor in theatre isn't very marketable, it turns out." Anita laughed nervously. "I went back and earned a teacher's certificate and landed a job teaching English and History at White Castle High School. I've been back in the area since the school year started."

"Do you want to meet after work someday soon and catch up?" Christie asked. "I haven't run into any of our other class-mates since I moved back home."

Anita smiled shyly. "I'd like that. I'll let you get back to work while I browse for a moment. I heard your aunt call you. I'll leave my number with her." Anita nodded toward the regis-ter. "I remember her from our high school days. She was always quite the character."

"Still is. Great to see you. My business card is on the desk, where you can sign up for email if you like. Or just take a card." The friends air-kissed and finger-waved at each other.

Christie smiled and said "Hi" and "Welcome" to browsing customers as she walked back through the shop. When she reached the main counter, she stopped and asked her aunt, "I heard you call me. Do you need something?"

Aunt Doris narrowed her eyes and said, "I just got off the phone with a gentleman who wants to order flowers with a certain message. He was talking about how he read on your website that some flowers have special meanings and hoped we could do that."

"You're the one who taught me the meanings of flowers when I was a teenager working here. What's the problem?"

"He wants to send someone flowers that relay the message, 'Be careful.'"

"Did he explain what he meant by that? Like to not get

hurt?"

"No, I think it was more that he was trying to tell someone to watch their back."

"Did he leave a name?"

"No to that as well. He's going to send someone to pick them up on Monday. He said it would be a 'Mr. Jones' and he'd pay with cash."

Christie arched an eyebrow. "Halloween's coming up next weekend. Maybe it's his idea of a prank."

Aunt Doris furrowed her brow. "I hope that's all it is."

Christie shrugged and circled back to some women who were giggling as they read the messages in the greeting cards in one of the racks. She recognized one of them as her mother's neighbor, Lettie Lesbitt, who had been her Girl Scout leader when Christie was in grade school. She interrupted the laughing long enough to thank Mrs. Lesbitt for teaching her basic camping skills. "I didn't know that would lead me to be the chief cook on most of the backpacking trips I did in college," she said.

Mrs. Lesbitt blushed and beamed. "Oh, Christie. I'm so glad you're back in town. So many of you bright young people leave forever."

"That was my plan A, but it looks like my life has taken a detour. So far, it's been great to be back in the community, though. Thanks for coming in," said Christie. She nodded at each of the women in turn. "I hope you'll come in again."

Christie excused herself and turned her attention to a nicely dressed woman who was admiring the cherry writing desk. It had graceful, turned legs, a wooden extension that folded out to create a larger writing surface, and a half dozen shallow drawers. Christie had imagined they would hold stamps or pens or even a thin sheaf of stationery.

"Hi. I'm Christie. May I help you with that desk?"

The attractive brunette looked up and smiled. "Well, yes. This is a very nice piece. I remember my grandmother having something like this in her dining room." She lovingly moved her fingers across the polished surface. "She used to sit and write letters to her relatives back in Italy. Back in the day when we all wrote real letters." She sighed and asked, "Do you still write letters?"

Christie shook her head. "Not unless you count the note I add to my Christmas cards every year. And the 'thank you' cards I write on occasion. My mother instilled that practice in me."

"I miss the handwritten notes. An email or text just isn't the same thing. Do you know anything about the desk?"

Christie shook her head. "I wish I could tell you, but I'm not sure about its provenance. It was already here when I took the shop over from my grandmother. I don't recognize it, so I'm pretty sure it came from someone outside my family."

"It's a nice piece. Even if it hadn't belonged to my grandmother, I would think of her when I use it." She smiled. "How much are you asking for it?"

Christie opened the top left drawer where she had tucked the price tag. "Three hundred dollars. I looked it up online and saw similar desks that were about that price."

The woman clicked her tongue as she opened several drawers and examined the writing extension.

"You wouldn't have to pay shipping as you would if you bought it on eBay," Christie continued. "Or, if you live in the area, I could deliver it to you if that would help. What is your name, if you don't mind my asking?"

"Lynette." She extended a hand, which Christie took, noticing the strength of her grip. "I want to buy it. Can you put a 'sold' sign on it, and I'll come by tomorrow and take care of the purchase?"

Christie started to open her mouth to ask for payment before agreeing to mark it as 'sold,' but instead, she smiled and said, "The shop will be closed tomorrow because it's Sunday, but I'll be happy to complete the deal on Monday."

The potential desk sale prompted Christie to ask her aunt about the note she'd found. She rummaged through her desk drawer to retrieve it and walked back to help her aunt with a flower arrangement and show her the letter.

Aunt Doris read the short message and pursed her lips. "I vaguely remember a bar fight back in the eighties when a man was hit with a pool cue and died a few days later. But I don't know who Missy or 'B' would have been."

"Do you remember the name of the man who died?"

Aunt Doris thought for a moment while inserting stems of eucalyptus into the vase. "Arnold something. Arnold Young-man. I remember because he was way too young to die, not an old man."

Christie smiled at her aunt's logic. "Anything else? Was he a local guy?"

"Yes, but he didn't live right in town. He was something of a scallywag and always in some kind of trouble. It seems like there was some question about another suspect who disappeared. The man who was convicted and sent to prison swore he was innocent. But there was never proof of anyone else."

Christie folded the note and put it back in the envelope. "I wonder who wrote this and sent it to Missy. And why was it in that desk?"

Aunt Doris glowered over her half-rim glasses. "Now, don't you go starting up any trouble, young lady. That was old business and doesn't concern you."

Christie started to respond, but her aunt's look stopped her. She wondered how much more there was to the story.

CHAPTER
THREE

Sunday morning, when Christie opened the back door to her shop, Stormy immediately jumped to the top shelf behind the sales counter. It was as though she knew that was the point from which she could keep an eye on all the goings-on. The grand reopening had been more successful than Christie had dared to hope. She and Aunt Doris had spent another hour after the five o'clock closing doing cleanup and getting the shop ready for Monday's normal day of business.

Christie spent her morning rearranging some of the displays and ordering replacement stock of gift items and cards. When she was done with that, she set about writing up the list of flowers she would need for the week ahead, both for the arrangements that had been ordered the previous day and for the drop-in customers. As she prepared the order for her aunt to place the next morning, she sensed her grandmother's presence in her heart. She felt sure she had made the right decision to be in the flower shop. She sighed and then, being the accountant that she was, dutifully recorded the sales from the previous business day in her digital ledger. When she was finished, she smiled to herself. It was a very nice number. Plus, Lynnette was coming by some time the next day to pay three hundred dollars for the writing desk. That would be a great start to her Monday's receipts.

Christie transferred the orders for the week onto a desktop calendar. It would help her aunt to see the workload for each day and would also make it easier to see how many deliveries would need to be made on any given day. She knew there would be add-ons during the week but hoped the calendar would keep things less chaotic.

She was pleasantly surprised a few minutes later to get a text message from Anita suggesting that they get together Tuesday evening at a newly opened pub in town. Christie dashed off a reply. She hadn't developed any close friendships with women (or men, she realized) during her ten years in San Francisco and looked forward to changing that in the smaller town. She found herself mentally going through her clothes closet, wondering if she had anything worthy of a pub date. Then she reminded herself it was just drinks with a girlfriend, not a real "date."

BY FIVE O'CLOCK, she was done with store business, and it was time to head to her parents' home. Christie had promised her mom that she would come over for dinner. Her mother greeted her with a warm hug and scratched Stormy behind the ears. "Your kitty is thriving now that she has a regular home and meals. Grandma Maude couldn't bring herself to officially adopt a full-time animal. She always said it would take too much time."

"I enjoy having her with me at the shop and at home, too." Christie nuzzled the cat. "She's really not a problem at all. Even Aunt Doris pets her now and then. And the customers seem to enjoy having her there. She doesn't bother anyone."

"Your aunt has a good heart, but she's never really been an animal person, as I recall."

"There was one guy that Stormy hissed at yesterday. Why, I don't know."

Mrs. O'Mara smiled and started to head to the kitchen. "It's hard to know why animals do what they do. So, anything new in the social world? Or are you too busy with the shop?"

"I got a text from an old friend earlier today. I'm meeting Anita Sanders at The Tap Room in a couple of days. You remember her, I'm sure. She and I played volleyball in high school."

"Didn't she go to Stanford? She was always pleasant, as I recall. How's business going so far?"

"Way better than I expected. Maybe it's just because I'm new, but I sure hope it continues. We'll have to wait and see." Christie took a bite of a fresh oatmeal raisin cookie offered by her mom. "Yum. Dinner smells good, by the way."

"I thought I'd fix your favorite stroganoff."

"No one makes it better than you."

Mrs. O'Mara beamed. "Tell me more about the shop."

Christie related several stories about interesting interactions, including the woman who wanted to buy the vintage desk. "Do you remember that pretty writing desk that we found in the closet and cleaned up for sale?"

"Yes. I recall that you were trying to decide whether or not to keep it in case it was a family heirloom. What about it?"

"Well, once you convinced me you'd never seen it before, I finished readying it for sale and found a note taped to the bottom of one of the drawers. It was written to a 'Missy' and seemed to be about a guy who died after a bar fight. It was from someone who signed it with the letter 'B.' Aunt Doris said it might have been about a man named Arnold Youngman. It had something to do with a bar fight back in the eighties, but she wouldn't tell me anything else. Do you have any idea about such an incident?"

"Well, I have no recollection whatsoever. I would have been too young back then." She opened the oven door. The tantalizing aroma of fresh bread filled the room.

"Smells delicious!"

"You can set the table while I dish up the food. And tell your father that dinner is ready."

A few minutes later, after saying grace, Mrs. O'Mara said, "I just thought of someone who might remember a bar fight. Jack Smith lived a couple of houses down from us. He would have been in his twenties at that time. He still lives in the same house — the gray one with white trim on the corner. You might ask him about it. But don't get your hopes up. That was a long time ago."

"Great idea, Mom. I'll check with him this evening after dinner."

THE FRONT PORCH light had either burned out or been turned off, but Christie saw lights on in a room in the back of the house. She guessed it was the kitchen or a family room. She pressed the doorbell but didn't hear a chime, so she knocked loudly and waited. After a moment or so, during which she asked herself if this had been a good idea in the first place, the porch light clicked on, and the door opened halfway. Standing in front of her was a frumpy-looking man with thin gray hair and wearing denim jeans with suspenders and a plaid shirt that had been buttoned askew.

"Who are you? I don't need any religious lectures, if that's why you're here."

He started to close the door, but Christie put her foot on the door jamb and said quickly, "Mr. Smith, I'm not selling anything. I'm your neighbor up the street, or at least my mom and dad are."

"Who are they?" He opened the door another inch or two.

"The O'Maras. Thomas and Maureen. Or maybe you remember my aunt, Doris O'Mara. She works at the flower shop downtown."

His face clouded over for a moment, then brightened. "I kinda remember the ladies at the flower shop. One of them had frizzy red hair."

Christie chuckled. "Yes, that would be my Aunt Doris."

"I'm Jack Smith, by the way."

"Christie O'Mara. Pleased to officially meet you." She offered a hand, which Jack shook vigorously.

"Well, what do you want?"

"I hoped you might remember a man named Arnold Youngman. He was in a bar fight in the early eighties and died a few days later. It seems like one of the men with whom he was fighting disappeared and was never charged with causing his death."

He straightened up a bit with what Christie assumed was family pride as he stated flatly, "My dad was a deputy sheriff back in those days. He talked about that case now and then. What made you start looking into it? Why does it matter now?" Mr. Smith frowned. "The evidence proved it was a guy named Bronco Carver, and he went to prison for it. And Arnold's been dead a long time."

"It's kind of a long story." Christie recited a brief synopsis of the desk and its letter. "So, I wondered if the name 'Missy' or a man whose name started with a 'B' — who might have been Bronco, or this mystery man, I suppose — might be connected to it."

His face tightened. "That Missy was a real looker. Every guy around wanted to take her out."

Christie felt her pulse quicken. "Do you remember her real name? Missy sounds like a nickname to me. And what about the guy?"

"Seems like her name was Teresa, but everyone called her Missy. She acted like she was all prim and proper, but she was always nice to everyone." His eyes darkened. "I never personally knew the other man you're talking about. Some of the locals said he was from up near Chehalis. There are a half dozen small towns in that direction. I'm sure he wasn't from here."

"Did Teresa have a last name?"

He snorted. "Doesn't everyone? Her last name was Stewart."

"Do you know what happened to her after Arnold died?"

"As I recollect, she left town soon after the big fight. Some people thought Arnold was having an argument with the man I just told you about. He disappeared, too."

"Do you remember if the mystery man was ever named as a suspect?"

Jack shook his head. "I don't rightly recall. It seems after a few weeks, the town just kinda forgot about the other man. I know the police looked for the other man for a while but gave up. It wasn't as easy then to search for people who wanted to hide. Bronco Carver was charged and went to prison. That's all I can remember."

"Is there someone else who might know more?" Christie asked.

"Maybe sometimes we should let sleeping dogs lie and not stir up the past," said Jack before closing the door and turning off the porch light.

CHAPTER

FOUR

Come Monday morning, clouds had formed overnight, and what started as a light mist had turned to rain. It was a perfect day to settle into the bramble of files her grandmother had left. And to ponder the note she'd found a couple of days earlier.

Aunt Doris shook her head when Christie asked if she remembered any more about Missy or B. "I surely don't know who they might be or were. This seems like an old-fashioned letter, to have been found this way. I mean, who writes real notes anymore? And why was it taped to the bottom of the desk drawer?"

"The lady who wanted to buy this desk on Saturday asked me the same question about writing notes, although I didn't tell her about this one. It certainly appears that B hand-delivered it."

"Or had someone else take it to Missy," said Aunt Doris.

Christie studied the note again, looking for an angle that might give some context for the message. "You mentioned that a bar fight happened in the eighties. I could look up old newspapers at the library and find out more information. "I don't suppose you recall how Grandma got the desk, do you?"

"Not right off, but I remember her saying that she planned to keep track of that kind of thing." She snickered. "Whether she did or not is another matter."

"I'm wondering if I should hang on to the desk until we find out who Missy was." Christie laid the envelope on her work desk.

"You could certainly keep the note. That lady wouldn't know there had been one unless you told her."

"That's a good point." Christie tucked the envelope into her back pocket. "I'll be sure to get Lynette's name and address in case I want to contact her later. But what if we find Missy, and *she* wants the desk back?"

Aunt Doris laughed. "Well, then she shouldn't have let it go in the first place. If it were me, I'd sell the desk and not worry a minute more about it."

"I suppose you're right. I probably won't find Missy, whoever she is, anyway." Christie shrugged and sat down behind the order desk.

She opened one of the two drawers in the file cabinet under the order counter where her grandmother had filed miscellaneous documents. She had previously found several useful files, including one containing receipts for major purchases dating back twenty years. Several bulging folders held the handwritten orders for all of the weddings and funerals and other worthy celebrations that had occurred over the previous forty years. Christie decided to move them to the back storage closet now that she had made room by moving out the furniture.

Grandma Maude had only recently started entering orders into her computer system. Aunt Doris explained that a few orders had been accidentally deleted during the early days of its use, so the two women decided to use a dual system. They wrote the original order longhand and then entered the necessary details into the computer system. It was a bit of extra work, but entering the key financial data made the bookkeeper happy, while the handwritten orders kept the customers happy. And provided a backup of orders if they hit a wrong button on the computer again.

Christie started sorting through the papers in the first of the two drawers. Most of them weren't in any particular order. She made a mental note to organize the files properly, being the accountant that she was. For the time being, her concern was to find any kind of record that might help her identify the origin of the writing desk and maybe lead to discovering the rest of the story behind the note.

In the meantime, Aunt Doris busied herself with preparing the bouquets and floral arrangements that had been ordered on Saturday. The flower delivery from the wholesale company wouldn't arrive until about eleven a.m., but Christie had ordered enough fresh stock the previous week that there were blooms left over from the grand reopening for the first half dozen orders.

Christie had finished searching through the first of the two drawers without finding anything remotely related to the desk or any other piece of furniture in the shop. She had barely started looking in the second drawer when her aunt called from the back room where she was creating one of her masterpieces. She walked over to see what was going on and stretch her legs at the same time after sitting in a semi-stooped position for a long hour. "What is it, Aunt Doris?"

"I'm fussing with that strange order that's supposed to send the message of 'Be careful' and I'm not sure which flowers to use. I wish I knew what the man meant by those words." She shook her head and handed the chart of flowers' meanings to her niece. "Which of these do you think would work best?"

Christie perused the list, smiling as she noted some of the traditional interpretations, such as cyclamen representing "it's over" or "goodbye," and violet meaning "modesty." She wondered if that had contributed to the origin of the term "shrinking violet." Looking at her aunt, she asked, "Did the customer tell you anything more? Do you think he knew the meanings himself?"

"He referred to the ad you have on Facebook that said something about flowers having special messages. I tried to explain to him that those meanings were from Victorian times and didn't mean much in today's world. But he still wanted to send a bouquet that had a hidden message."

"Hmm. It won't mean anything to the recipient if that person doesn't know about the old Victorian traditions. I suppose we could include a chart of possible meanings, but if it's supposed to be hidden, that wouldn't be apropos, I suppose."

Aunt Doris tilted her head and looked at Christie with a raised eyebrow over the top of the half-glasses that she wore when working with flowers.

"On second thought, I think we should go with a combination of white stephanotis for good luck and the yellow and black black-eyed Susans for encouragement," said Christie. "I'm going with the presumption that the caller was trying to convey a message of staying safe instead of warning of danger."

"That's certainly not the feeling I got when I had him on the phone." Her face hardened. "Rhododendron represents 'beware,' but those would be hard to put into a vase."

Christie smiled at her aunt. "I'd like to keep this on a positive note. Let's just make it pretty. The recipient isn't likely to know what the flowers mean, and I'm not sure the sender would ever see them anyway."

Aunt Doris shrugged and picked the proper stems from the buckets of water in the refrigerated case. "Works for me. I'll fill it out with eucalyptus and yellow carnations — which mean disappointment, if you recall — and it will be lovely. The message will be balanced, if you will, between wishing success and preparing for despair."

Christie agreed with a nod. "I'll fill out the sales receipt for you before I get back to that second file drawer. So far, I haven't had any luck finding any of Grandma's records on the furniture."

"Try looking for a folder labeled 'vintage' because that's how she talked about that kind of stuff. She said none of it was old enough to be legitimate antiques, but it didn't matter because vintage is so popular right now."

"You're assuming these files are actually in alphabetical order," said Christie with a giggle. "Some aren't labeled at all, but they will be by the time I'm done reorganizing them later this week. It will make it so much easier to find things."

The two women worked companionably for the next half hour. The phone rang several times, and Christie listened as Aunt Doris took a couple of orders for birthday flowers and a "thank you" arrangement. As the lunch hour neared, Christie sent her aunt home for a lunch break and manned the shop on her own. She was pleased that a half dozen customers came in, possibly also on their lunchtimes, and purchased cards and gift items.

She knew her financial success would come more from sufficient sales of the ancillary items than from the sale of flowers. She'd done some research before opening the business, and so far, after two days of actual business, she was feeling optimistic that everything would work out as she'd hoped. Her customers were buying cards, boxes of note cards with clever sayings, and small items like glass angels and other trinkets. She was still searching through the second file drawer when the door chimed to alert her that a customer had entered. Christie looked up to see Lynette standing just inside the door, her eyes scanning the room. Lynette's shoulders relaxed when she saw Christie stand up from behind the counter.

"Hi," said Christie. "I presume you're here for that writing desk."

"Yes. I trust you didn't sell it out from under me." Lynette's mouth smiled, but it didn't reach her eyes.

"I put a 'sold' sign on it so other customers would know it was already spoken for. Are you going to pay for it with cash or a card today?"

"Didn't I pay for it Saturday?"

"No, you didn't. I remember thinking that I should have completed the purchase before marking it 'sold,' but you had an honest face, and we were swamped at the moment."

"Yes, of course. You're right." Lynette pulled out a credit card from her handbag. "That was two hundred dollars, wasn't it?"

Christie shook her head and showed her the price tag, which she retrieved from the desk's top drawer. "No, it was *three* hundred dollars. Shall I ring it up for you?"

Lynette's face didn't flinch. She handed the Visa card to Christie and said, "Go ahead."

Christie entered the details into her business iPad and slid the card into the slot. She frowned and repeated the process. She pursed her lips and tried a third time. "I'm sorry. This card is not processing. Do you have another one I can try?" She handed the card back, but not before noticing Lynette's last name: Nichols.

Lynette fumbled in her wallet for a long moment before asking, "May I write a check?"

Christie would normally have taken a check for a purchase from a local customer, but she sensed a tenuous bank account balance and wasn't certain of Ms. Nichols' reliability, given their conversation so far. She had to come up quickly with a reason for declining. She smiled and shook her head, saying, "I wish I could, but my bank isn't allowing checks yet, or even Venmo or Zelle, because my shop is a new account. I can only accept cash or credit card for the time being. I hope you can understand that. Can you return with cash, perhaps? I'll save the desk until tomorrow for you."

Lynette pursed her lips before finally saying, "Yes, I'll do that. Thank you. I'll come in tomorrow morning."

Christie watched as Ms. Nichols left the shop and climbed into the passenger seat of a late-model Porsche waiting in the parking lot. "Why wouldn't she be able to afford that desk if she's getting into an expensive car?" Christie asked Stormy, who had awakened from her nap and was strutting across the top of the desk. "And how did she think she was going to fit it into that car?"

CHAPTER
FIVE

"Ah ha!" exclaimed Christie, holding a battered manila folder in her hands.

Stormy opened an eye, and Aunt Doris asked, "Did you find what you were looking for?" She had finished putting the fresh flowers from the supply company in the refrigerated case and had started building one of the arrangements that had been ordered earlier in the day.

"Maybe. Grandma apparently used this folder for miscellaneous things that didn't fit any of her other categories. I found a couple of notes that seem to refer to that curio wall cabinet on the back wall and a corner cabinet that I sold on Saturday. I'm still looking for a reference to the writing desk."

"Were you able to convince your mom's neighbor girl to do some deliveries for the shop?" Aunt Doris tucked a few more blossoms into a birthday bouquet meant for a sixteen-year-old girl. The soft pink roses, white baby's breath and darker pink carnations were lovely, with a backdrop of dark green foliage and a few spires of olive-green eucalyptus. "This one will be ready to go in a few minutes."

"Heather said she could deliver for us after school a couple of days a week. Luckily, today is one of them. I figured I could do some of them myself as well when I need to."

"When your grandmother had the shop, a lot of customers picked up their own orders. Small town people don't expect delivery service like in the big cities."

Christie nodded. "Or maybe they don't want to pay a delivery fee. But I'll have to charge something to cover my costs, even if I don't really want to."

Aunt Doris scoffed. "Well, it's not like they can expect us to offer free service like Amazon Prime. Which, really, they pay for anyway, but at a yearly fee. However, few of them pay attention to that. They only see the 'free delivery' angle."

Christie nodded, then turned her attention back to the file drawer. A few minutes later, she said, "I think I found something. Look at this, Aunt Doris."

Christie laid the handwritten note which was scrawled on a piece of ecru stationery on her desk, and read it aloud to her aunt.

This writing desk belonged to my grandmother. She died when I was very small, but my mother told me stories about it being jinxed, so Mom eventually stored it in our attic instead of displaying and using it. I'm moving to a retirement home and don't have a place for it.

Maybe you can sell it to someone who will love it.

"There's no name anywhere on this," said Aunt Doris. "And it doesn't specify that it's a cherry desk. It may not be the same one after all."

"True, but it's the only clue I have at the moment. Maybe it belonged to Missy's grandmother."

"I suppose that's a possibility, but how do you think you'll manage to find this Missy person anyway?"

Christie leaned with her elbows on top of the counter. "I could try searching the old White Castle newspapers. I remember Mom saying that the local papers used to have columns about all the local news and gossip, like 'Mrs. Davis hosted the White Castle Women's Club for their January meeting. She served pineapple cake and homemade ice cream' and stuff like that."

"That's true. But that was a lot of years ago, and there are years and years of old issues to go through. Even our local weekly publication would mean fifty-two papers a year." Aunt Doris snipped a few stems for the next bouquet.

"I could pretend I'm on a scavenger hunt." Christie grinned, then shrugged as she considered the mountainous task. "It's not important, I guess. Missy and B could be from another city or state for all we know." Christie tucked the letter into a manila folder of paperwork, which she planned to take home with her.

The door chimed. Heather bounced into the shop with a big smile on her face. "Hi, Miss O'Mara. Hi, Aunt Doris. Mom said you called and had a couple of deliveries for me."

Christie extended a hand. "You can call me Christie. Miss O'Mara sounds old. Like what strangers might call Aunt Doris."

Aunt Doris harrumphed. "There are no strangers in White Castle. Everyone calls me Aunt Doris."

Heather giggled. "That's funny. I don't even think of you as having a last name. You've always been 'Aunt Doris' to my family and me. And everyone in town, like you said."

Aunt Doris had secured the two floral arrangements for delivery in cardboard carriers and printed the addresses for Heather. "These are both close to town. Call if you have any problems along the way."

"And please text me when you're on your way home so I know the deliveries are done and that you're safe," said Christie.

Once Heather was out the door, Christie said to her aunt, "I can manage the shop by myself if you'd like to go home early. The phone's been quiet the last hour, and I doubt we'll have any more traffic late on a Monday afternoon, especially with this rain."

Aunt Doris hugged her niece and donned her hooded raincoat, necessary attire for the rainy fall weather on the western side of the Cascades in the Pacific Northwest. "I'll be here early tomorrow and get started on all those flowers for Mr. Hallstrom's funeral. I would expect there will probably be a few more orders in the morning, him being a longtime resident and all."

After spiffing up the shop in readiness for Tuesday, Christie turned her attention to searching for archived issues of the city's *White Castle Gazette* online. Although the newspaper had been published since 1906, the only available issues online were from 1997 to 1999. She perused the weekly editions despite the probability that they were too recent to be useful. And they were. She would have to go to the local library to see if they had additional issues on microfiche or perhaps even the original papers.

She was hunkered at her desk, studying one of the reference lists of the meaning of certain flowers, when the door chime chirped. A man who appeared to be in his fifties or sixties looked to his right and left as he entered, then approached the order desk, whereupon he looked around again. "Anyone here?" he called. He jumped when Christie stood up and asked, "How can I help you?" from her desk. She had been out of his line of sight.

He stammered. "I-I thought the shop was empty for a moment there. Yes, I'm here to pick up some flowers that were called in on Saturday."

"Do you have a name so I can find the order?" Christie was fairly certain this had to be the man who was to pick up the special arrangement with the message, "Be Careful," as it was the only one left in the glass case.

"My friend said it would be labeled for pick up by Mr. Jones. Do you have it ready?"

"I'll get it from the cabinet. My aunt prepared it for you this morning."

Mr. Jones tapped his fingernails on the counter. Stormy stood up from her perch on the top shelf and jumped down. She landed directly in front of the man, arched her back and hissed at him. He stepped backward and shrieked. "It's a black cat. That's bad luck!"

Christie had witnessed the moment and chuckled under her breath. "Stormy's my shop cat. She might think she's protecting me." She set the flowers on the counter and picked up the cat, who purred in her arms. "She's harmless," she said as she kissed Stormy on the nose before setting her down.

"What do I owe you?"

"That'll be sixty-two dollars and fifty-three cents. Cash or card?" Transaction completed in cash, Christie secured the vase in a sturdy container for transport and offered to carry it to her customer's car, but he declined. She watched him as he left in his black SUV. She couldn't help but notice his license plate number — B7WG666 — and wondered if he was superstitious about the triple six, considering his reaction to her black cat. She looked at her cat. Stormy had been pleasant to everyone who had come into the shop. Why did she hiss at Mr. Jones?

CHAPTER

SIX

After a bite of dinner for herself and kibble for the cat, Christie left Stormy curled up on the small sofa and headed to the local library. She was happy to discover that it stayed open till seven a couple of evenings each week. That would give her a good hour to search through the old papers, assuming the library had any. She'd forgotten to ask when she called, but surely they would have some on microfiche, she figured.

The reading room at the White Castle Public library was well-lit. The bright white LED lights helped to dispel the otherwise gloomy nature of the large space that was filled with rows of shelves of reference books of all kinds, plus a couple of racks of newspapers. The librarian had given Christie brief instructions on how to use the microfiche file, apologizing for the lack of indexing. "We're just too small to have the budget to digitalize them." She smiled and said, "Good luck, dear," before she hustled back to the main desk.

Christie mentally debated looking for the death of a young man within the years her aunt mentioned versus looking for the name Missy or Teresa Stewart. When she realized that Missy was more likely some young girl's nickname and might have been a popular one at that, she chose to search for a bar fight or the name of Arnold Youngman. And crossed her fingers for good luck, although she wasn't really superstitious.

About forty-five minutes later, she had scanned a mere two years' worth of the weekly paper. She had decided to start at 1979 based on only her aunt's recollections to guide her. At twenty or so minutes per year of print and with ten years of publications in the eighties alone, she calculated she could potentially search for at least three hours. She shook her head, gulped down some water and opened the next year's microfiche file of newspapers.

A half hour later, in the April 16, 1982, issue, she found a short article about a young man having died after a bar fight in the Paradise Saloon. Several men had gotten into a brawl. When the police arrived, they found the victim on the floor with abrasions and a an apparent head injury. Two of the witnesses reported that one of the other men had hit the man with a pool cue in the back of the head. He wasn't named, but a week later, a follow-up story reported that a second suspect had been identified but had left the area. She scanned the next several editions and found a reference to a trial that was to start in another month. A man named Bronco Carver was going to be tried for the death of Arnold Youngman, who had died three days after said bar fight.

She skimmed through the next couple of months' worth of papers and found a follow-up story in the June 25 edition, two months after the original story. The trial was to start in the county courthouse the following Monday. With a trickle of anticipation, she eagerly read a long article about the trial in the following week's edition. Mr. Carver had been found guilty of homicide, although he staunchly denied that he had been the one who had used the pool cue. Unfortunately, he was unable to identify who that other person might have been. He was sentenced to twenty-five years in prison.

She checked the time and noticed that it was only ten minutes until the library would close. And her eyes were tired from staring at the small screen for the past hour. She picked up her material and went to the desk, where she requested a copy of the articles to pick up the next day. As she headed out into the stormy weather, she wondered if the second suspect had ever been located and if his name also started with a "B." She considered her next move during the short drive to her home.

TUESDAY MORNING STARTED with sunshine and broken clouds — an unusual but welcome weather phenomenon in late October. Halloween fell on Friday, three days away. Christie was sure that most parents were hoping for a dry day for the sake of the little ones who would be out trick-or-treating. In addition to keeping them dry, it would also make it safer because children were easier to see when it wasn't raining.

The phone was busy with Aunt Doris taking numerous orders for boutonnieres and corsages for a Halloween-themed party at the high school Saturday night. Her aunt's prediction of more orders for the funeral that afternoon was correct. Christie helped her aunt with a half dozen arrangements that she would deliver herself to the church prior to the service, which was scheduled for one o'clock.

Lynette didn't show up during the morning hours. Christie decided that if Lynette failed to show by the end of the day, she would mark the desk as "not for sale" and keep it as a display piece.

Christie went to the library after delivering the funeral

flowers to the church and picked up the articles she had requested. She hustled back to the shop to read them more thoroughly and to help her aunt with the orders that had been coming in all morning. She had checked the inventory of fresh flowers and realized she didn't have nearly enough for the corsages that had been ordered so far. She placed an order for more carnations, baby's breath, and yellow and pink roses, which would arrive on Friday. She smiled, happy that business so far had been great.

She turned her attention to looking up the public records for deaths in the county. She quickly discovered it wouldn't be as easy as she thought. Having grown up in a world where the internet had existed from her childhood, she hadn't considered the possibility that a death in 1982 might not be so easy to find in an online search. Couldn't Google find everything? She had a name, Arnold L. Youngman, but no other identifying data such as birth date. The brief article in the paper was sadly skimpy on such important details. She found an online company that offered death certificates for a price. It listed a dozen pieces of information required before someone could order one, though — information she didn't have. Christie found herself at a dead-end for the moment.

She decided to ask her aunt one more time about the man who died. Aunt Doris's halo of wispy, carrot-red hair seemed to bristle as she said, "He was a no-good kid. Got himself in trouble for one thing or another all the time. He probably deserved whatever happened to him." With that, she went back to making an autumn-themed arrangement for some lucky person with an upcoming birthday.

Sensing a touchy subject, Christie tucked the news pieces into her tote bag. She planned to stop by her parents' house on her way home and would ask them if they knew anything.

When it was time to close, the writing desk hadn't been

claimed, and Christie removed the "sold" sign from it. She was secretly glad that Lynette hadn't shown up. She was determined to learn the real story behind the mysterious note and reasoned that even if keeping the desk didn't help her find it, seeing it would be a bit of incentive to keep digging. She realized there was no logic in her reasoning, but her sixth sense was happy with her decision.

CHAPTER

SEVEN

Christie left the shop, Stormy in tow, with plans to stop by to see her parents for a quick minute before heading home to change clothes for her rendezvous with Anita. Her mother greeted her with a big hug and scratched Stormy under the chin. "How's your kitty doing at the shop?"

"I enjoy having her with me at work and at home, too." Christie kissed the cat's nose. She frowned a moment as she recalled, "There was one guy who Stormy hissed at yesterday. Why, I don't know."

"Hmm. Well, we're glad to see you both. Are you staying for dinner?" Maureen O'Mara started to head to the kitchen.

"No, Mom. I'm meeting Anita Sanders at The Tap Room in a few minutes." She followed her mother into the kitchen, where her mother had just opened the oven door. The tantalizing aroma of roast beef filled the room.

"Smells delicious! I wish I were staying for dinner."

"I'll save you some to heat up for an easy meal." Maureen began plating the roast and potatoes and carrots.

"Thanks, Mom. I'll come by tomorrow after work to rescue my leftovers and tell you about my visit with Anita. Tell Dad I said 'Hi' and that I'm sorry I missed him." Christie kissed her mom on the cheek and popped back out into the chilly evening air to drive to her own home.

CHRISTIE STARED at the clothes in her closet, wondering what she should wear for a girl's night out in the small town. She wished she knew what Anita would be wearing. She wondered if Anita would be dressed more upscale, having only recently moved from Seattle. With a sigh, she decided to go with skinny jeans with a black, long-sleeved, V-neck T-shirt, and a red leather jacket cut in the trendy motorcycle style. She added a favorite pair of black boots with two-inch heels and a chunky, silver-tone necklace. The reflection in her closet mirror gave its silent approval.

The Tuesday evening crowd at The Tap Room was on the small side, but it was only six o'clock and would likely get bigger as the hour got later. Christie found Anita sitting at a high-top table along the far wall. Anita hopped down from the stool and greeted her friend with European-style pecks, a habit leftover from spending a year abroad in France during college, she'd said.

The two friends laughed when they noticed each other's outfits. They had both gone the way of the middle road.

"I guess jeans, T-shirts and a jacket are safe choices everywhere," said Christie.

Anita smiled and nodded, saying, "We are so middle American!"

The waitress, Robin, sported several colors of hair — blue, purple, yellow — and multiple piercings. She took their order for a couple of pints of draft pale ale and told them of the evening's food special. It was "Taco Tuesday" at the pub with a special of two tacos for a dollar and a pint of beer at a dollar off. Very budget-friendly. After ordering chicken tacos, Anita and Christie chatted about jobs and the weather until the waitress returned with two mugs of beer.

"Here's to life in a small town," said Christie.

"Amen to that," replied Anita as they clinked glasses and took that first swallow.

"How's teaching at our alma mater working out for you?" asked Christie. "Do you find it hard to be in those same rooms we sat in over a decade ago?"

"Not really. The interior of the entire building was painted recently. And I think even the floor is new in the wing where my room is. Everything looks different anyway. My biggest challenge is being in front of those impressionable students and not being very much older than they are. I sometimes feel like I'm barely ahead of them in the subject matter. Almost every evening, I study and write notes for the next day or two." Anita took a long swallow of her beer.

"I would guess that's the case for most first-year teachers. Your second year will be a lot easier, I'm sure. Maybe even the second quarter will be easier." Christie moved her glass to make room for the twin baskets of tacos that Robin placed between Anita and her.

"It's second quarter already. Maybe it'll feel smoother by the time *third* quarter comes around." She giggled. "At least I'm teaching two of my favorite subjects from high school: history and theatre. I definitely had to bone up on history when I did my master's in education. Teaching it is different than reading about it. I used to wonder what it would have been like to live in a castle in the old days in Scotland or England, or even France. Theatre is easier. I acted in several plays on campus, so I have some practical personal experience.”

“Maybe you should have been an actress.”

Anita shook her head vigorously. “Oh, I couldn’t do that. I’ve discovered I’m much too timid for that. But in my fantasies, I can do anything.” She winked. “These tacos are just right on a cold evening. I’m glad you suggested coming here.”

“Good price and decent food. Should be good for keeping their business alive.”

“And I’m not likely to run into any of my students here. None of them are twenty-one yet.”

“There is that,” agreed Christie.

Tacos consumed, beer half-gone, Christie asked Anita, “Do you happen to recall someone named Lynette Nichols?”

Anita arched an eyebrow and tossed her mane of brown hair with tinted golden highlights. “I think there was a senior named Lynette the year we were freshmen, but her last name was Somers. I identified with her because she moved to White Castle her senior year. I remember thinking it had to be even harder to move to a new town as a senior. It was hard enough as a freshman. Why do you ask?”

“At the grand reopening on Saturday, a woman named Lynette Nichols came into the shop. She wanted to buy a writing desk that I’d found in the back room. When she came in on Monday to pick it up, she tried to claim she’d paid for it, and then she quoted a lower price when I informed her she hadn’t paid for it yet. I had to show her the price tag, which was a hundred dollars more. Then her credit card bounced, and that’s when I noticed her last name. She offered to write a check, but I asked for cash or a different card. Anyway, she left in a newer Porsche — she was the passenger — after telling me she would come in the next day, which would have been today, to get it. And she didn’t show up.”

"So, can't you just sell the desk to someone else?"

"Yes, and I've actually decided to keep it for the shop. But that isn't the problem. After the way she tried to do business with me, I'd say something about her is off. She wanted me to believe she'd paid for the desk when she hadn't and quoted a lower price than I'd told her. And her card bounced." Christie raised a brow. "I just hope she doesn't come back around."

EIGHT

When Christie arrived Wednesday morning to open for business, Aunt Doris was already busily fiddling with the flowers that would make up the bouquets that had been ordered to be delivered that day.

"Good morning, Christie," she called from the back of the shop. "How was your visit with your friend?"

"Hey, it was great. I think we'll be getting together regularly. It was almost like we'd kept in touch for the last fifteen years, even though we hadn't."

"That's a sign of a strong friendship, my child." Aunt Doris's thin fringe of red curls seemed to glow like an iridescent halo as she smiled at her favorite niece. "What did you find to talk about?"

"Lots of things. I even asked her if she knew Lynette, and she said she remembered a Lynette from school because she felt sorry for her having to transfer in during her senior year. Anita moved here when we were freshmen."

"Did she recall anything helpful about her other than that?"

"No. I'll have to dig up my high school yearbook from that year. Hopefully, she moved here in time for her class picture to be taken and was included in the album; then I'll know if she is the same person. Besides, it would be good to refresh my memory of all my old friends from school. I thought I'd go by Mom and Dad's house and find it after work. I need to pick up my leftovers anyway."

"Your mom will be happy to see you. You realize how much she's enjoying having you back in town, don't you?"

Christie nodded, her fingers busy making a ribbon bow for the vase her aunt was filling with flowers and foliage. "I hadn't realized how much I missed the small-town atmosphere in White Castle. And how nice it is to be able to see my parents and favorite aunt as often as I want without having to take vacation time and fly home." She turned and looked at her aunt. "And I don't have to cozy up to anyone superior to me just to keep a job. I like being in charge of my own success and future." She reached for another spool of ribbon. "Do you think Grandma Maude is happy I'm here?"

"I know she is. She often expressed her wish that you were here working in the shop. You have a natural talent, you know, for working with people. And flowers." Aunt Doris stepped back to admire her creation. "Done! What do you think? This one is for the president's secretary at Old National Bank. I'm guessing it's her birthday. Or maybe it's Secretary's Week, or whatever title is politically correct these days."

"It's gorgeous, Aunt Doris. She'll love it."

Christie tidied up the mess, then headed back to the front of the shop when she heard the sound of the door chime alerting her that someone was coming in.

A police officer stepped through the door and quickly scanned the room. Spotting Christie, he walked toward her desk.

"I'm Chief Conway. Are you the owner of this business?"

Christie felt her heart thumping like a racehorse in her chest. "Yes, that would be me. How can I help you?"

"Is your name Maude O'Mara?" he asked after consulting his notebook.

"No, Chief. My name is *Christie* O'Mara. Maude was my grandmother. This was her shop until she died a couple of months ago. Why do you ask?"

He reached into his shoulder pack and pulled out a Ziploc bag. He turned it over to show Christie. Inside was a small florist card and an envelope that read "Christie's Flower Shoppe."

Christie felt her face pale. "Is there a problem, Chief?"

"This was found at the home of a man who was found dead earlier today. It was on the counter next to a bouquet of flowers." He pulled up a photo of the flowers and held it out for Christie to examine. "Do you recognize these?"

Christie gasped. "Yes, I do, unfortunately. This was an arrangement that was specially ordered by a client over the phone last Saturday."

"I need any information you may have, such as a name and phone number."

Christie shook her head slowly. "I'm afraid I don't know anything about the gentleman who ordered the flowers. He didn't give a name and said he was sending someone else to pick them up. And that man paid cash."

"Telephone number?"

Christie shook her head again. "No, sir."

The officer narrowed his eyes. "So, you took an order without any identification or contact information?"

Christie nodded. "There isn't anything unusual about that in my business. But there was one thing that was odd."

"What was that?"

"My aunt took the order over the phone, and she said he wanted a special message conveyed through the flowers. You know, like red roses mean passionate love and yellow carnations mean disappointment."

"What message did he request?" The officer's brow furrowed.

"He wanted the bouquet to have a message of 'beware,' which I took to mean 'be careful,' although Aunt Doris believed he meant something more sinister."

"I see." The officer scribbled something in his spiral notebook.

Aunt Doris, hearing her name, joined the conversation. "He definitely meant something more like 'Watch your back.'"

"But I thought maybe he was planning to play a Halloween trick or something," said Christie.

"You didn't hear the tone of his voice as I did," said Aunt Doris.

Conway nodded, his lips pinched together. "What do you remember about the man who picked up the order?"

Christie thought for a moment. "He was at least fiftyish, brown hair, maybe five-foot-ten with a medium build. And he seemed jumpy. He asked for the flowers that were to be picked up by a 'Mr. Jones' — that's the name that the caller had given to Aunt Doris — but I'm sure that was a false name. He paid cash and left the little bit of change on the counter."

"Any distinguishing marks like a tattoo, or a mustache or maybe an accent?"

"Um. He wore a driving hat. You know, like you see in a British television program when someone's driving a convertible. It seemed out of place for White Castle, especially with the recent weather change. But no mustache or tattoos. He was wearing a trench coat and struck me as someone who looked like he would work in an office. Oh, and he was driving a dark

BMW SUV. License was…" Christie frowned a moment before recalling the number. "I don't remember the whole thing, but I remember wondering if he was superstitious because the last three digits were 666. Some people think that's an unlucky number."

"Hmm." Conway scribbled another note. "You don't take information on orders, but you notice license plate numbers?" He looked directly at her, and she realized the seeming incongruity of her actions. It made her a little, well, antsy to be second-guessed — and by a policeman, of all people.

"No, not usually. But a BMW is a bit pricey for White Castle, so I took an extra look at it. And the triple sixes, well, they just stood out to me."

She decided to turn questions back on him. "Can you tell me the name of the man who died?"

Conway folded his notebook and put it away in his jacket pocket "Not at this time. If I have any more questions, I'll be in touch with you."

Stormy jumped down from her perch on the top of the cabinet and landed on the counter next to Christie.

"Nice cat," said Conway, reaching out to scratch the kitty behind its ear.

"I just remembered something else," said Christie. "Stormy, that's my cat, hissed at the man when he picked up the flowers. She normally likes everyone." The officer gave her a quizzical look as if wondering what point she was making. Christie twirled her hair with her fingers and just shrugged.

～

"THIS GETS CURIOUSER AND CURIOUSER, to quote from *Alice in Wonderland,*" said Christie after the police chief left. "I wish I knew who died."

"I wonder if it's someone we know. It'll be in the paper in the next day or two anyway," said her aunt. "I'm feeling a bit guilty, seeing as how maybe we somehow played a role in his death."

"Oh, Aunt Doris. You know our bouquet didn't have anything to do with his dying. Whoever ordered the flowers might have been sending him a reminder, you know, or someone was just worried about him. We don't know what he really meant with his message."

"That's just it. Maybe it was the killer who ordered them. Maybe if we hadn't agreed to send the flowers, he wouldn't have died. Maybe the man who picked them up really was the same man as the caller, and you were face-to-face with a killer!" Aunt Doris threw up her hands and stomped back to her work table.

Christy shook her head at her drama queen aunt. "Well, I know for certain that we didn't send deadly flowers. I *would* like to know how he died, however."

"Well, we aren't going to find that out, young lady. Conway wasn't about to tell you when he was here. It's probably confidential information while the death is being investigated."

Christie smiled with a glint in her eye. "There's got to be someone who knows." She wiped some water from the counter. "Maybe Mom or Dad knows something. I need to stop by anyway to find my yearbook and to visit with Mom's neighbors who might remember Arnold Youngman."

"It doesn't really matter, you know," said Aunt Doris. "Arnold died a long time ago."

"I'd still like to know the rest of the story. Especially if it has something to do with the desk."

NINE

Christie coaxed Stormy into her carrier and locked up the store. The weather was typical for late October, with dark skies, clouds, and intermittent rain showers. Just right for a ghostly atmosphere for trick-or-treating in a couple of days, she thought to herself. And for murder. She shivered involuntarily. Rain in huge drops started falling just as she pulled into her parents' driveway.

"Hi, Mom. Hi, Dad." Christie peeled off her raincoat and set Stormy free in the kitchen. "Smells good. Am I staying for dinner?"

Her mom laughed. "I have those leftovers for you, but you're welcome to join us for lasagna if you like. And fresh sourdough bread."

"I'd like that. Need any help?"

"No, I have it under control."

"Okay. I'm going to look for a yearbook in my room. Be back down in a few minutes."

Stormy followed Christie up the stairs to her bedroom. It still looked much like she had left it when she headed to college. She smiled as her eyes took in the turquoise and purple bedspread and the quilt that Grandma Maude had made for her. Some of the squares had been made of fabric left over from dresses also made by her grandmother. Stormy curled up in the very center of the bed. It was as though she knew that it was her special place.

The yearbooks stood silently in place on the shelf above her desk. She reached for the album dated 2003, her first year of high school as a freshman. First, she scrolled to the section of her own class photos. She smiled as she noticed the clothing trends of the day. She was certain the outfit she'd worn that day was hanging in the closet across the room, never to be in style again. It would stay there for now. Anita's photo stood out from the others — even then, she had a more cosmopolitan, more ethereal aura than all the other girls.

Next, she thumbed through the senior class photos, specifically looking for Lynette Somers. At the time Christie was in high school, she knew all of her own classmates, many of whom had started kindergarten together in the small town. It was the same for the class just ahead of hers and the class one year behind. Other than that, she didn't know as many of the students in other classes unless they happened to be an older or younger sibling of one of her friends.

That's what happened in towns where class sizes were only sixty to seventy students, in general. White Castle had grown significantly since then as people tired of the growth in the Portland-Vancouver metro area or were pushed out of the home buying market. They had moved north along Interstate 5, eventually reaching even White Castle, which was fifty miles north of the big city complex. And the schools in the towns along the way had exploded with new students.

Christie found Lynette's picture in the senior class gallery but didn't see any photos of her among the candid shots or in the pictures of the sports teams, pep club, or other on-campus organizations. Maybe she wasn't a joiner, or maybe she transferred in too late to be in any of the group shots. Christie snapped a photo with her cell phone to show Anita the next time she saw her. However, the girl in the yearbook photo didn't look much like the woman at the store. She also realized that the woman she thought was Lynette Nichols looked ten years older than she ought to if she had graduated only three or four years ahead of Christie and Anita. Her hopes plunged when she had to admit that this most likely wasn't the right Lynette. Christie decided to show Anita the photo anyway, although Anita hadn't recently seen Lynette in real life, as Christie had.

Her task done, she and the kitty headed back downstairs to the aroma of lasagna fresh from the oven. Christie allowed her mom to coerce her into eating a second helping of the delicious meal, including a dessert of pistachio gelato, before she headed home.

TEN

Christie settled into the old-fashioned, high-backed chair that she'd rescued from her grandmother's home, her feet tucked under her and Stormy purring on her lap. Her mind drifted to thinking about Missy and B and Arnold Youngman. And Jack Smith. What had he meant about "letting sleeping dogs lie?" She wondered if someone else in town might know more about the rest of the story. But who? She might have to visit nursing homes to find that one person.

Instead, she called Anita.

"I found my high school yearbooks and looked up Lynette Somers. She wasn't in any of them except in the individual photos, so you may be right about her moving here later in her senior year. But that's all I know about her so far."

"She would have graduated about eighteen years ago," said Anita.

"That's not that long ago. Do you think any of the office staff or maybe the principal would know what happened to her?"

"If there hasn't been complete turnover in the high school office since then, we might have a chance of finding someone who knows something. Do you want me to check tomorrow when I'm at the school?"

"That would be lovely," said Christie. "Thank you."

"Did you get a chance to talk to that neighbor your mother mentioned?"

"Yeah. His name is Jack Smith. He's older than I thought. I forget that people don't stay the same age as you remember." She giggled. "But I never really knew him back then. He was just a neighbor down the street who didn't interact with the rest of us."

"And what did you find out?"

"He told me that the girl named Missy was actually Teresa Stewart, and she was dating a young man from somewhere around Chehalis. He didn't remember the man's name, but he said they both disappeared shortly after the bar fight where Arnold Youngman was killed. In the paper, I read that they convicted a guy named Bronco Carver, so it's technically solved, except he claimed to be innocent."

"Why do you care?" Anita said with an edge to her voice. "You don't know these people, and they're probably long gone anyway. They could even be dead themselves."

"True, but justice doesn't have a time limit. Does it?"

"I guess not," Anita agreed.

"Oh! Something else! A policeman came to the shop today and asked me about some flowers that we sold. It was the bouquet whose flowers were supposed to imply the message, 'Be Careful.' The person who got them was found dead, so of course, they found the flowers with my business card and showed up at the shop."

"That must have been a little unnerving," said Anita. "What did you say?"

"I assured him that the flowers weren't deadly and explained about the strange caller who had ordered them."

"Do you know who died?"

"He wouldn't tell me, but the whole town will know by tomorrow. I hope there isn't a headline in the newspaper about 'killer flowers' or anything like that." Christie chuckled nervously.

"It's free advertising," quipped Anita.

"Not the kind I like."

"Hey. I have to finish my prep for tomorrow's classes, so I'm going to sign off. I'll ask about Lynette at the high school office. Good luck with your mysteries."

Christie scooted the cat from her lap and poured herself a glass of Baileys over ice. She sat at her desk and wrote a list of things she knew about the desk and Lynette and Missy. It wasn't much. Hopefully, someone would remember Missy — who was really Teresa Stewart — this many years later. She'd ask her Aunt Doris now that she had Missy's real name; she had lived in White Castle all her adult life. Tracking down Lynette should be easier, in theory, since she had lived here more recently. Christie considered whether Lynette knew about the note in the desk but thought it was more likely that she didn't. How could she?

CHAPTER

ELEVEN

Aunt Doris was all business when Christie walked into the shop the next morning. She snipped flower and foliage stems with fervor and stabbed them into the burgundy vase on the worktable in front of her.

"You don't get the paper, do you, honey?" Doris looked up from her work with an arched brow. "I brought this morning's copy for you. It's on your desk."

Christie set Stormy on her perch and grabbed the morning newspaper. The headline story above the fold on the first page was about a man who had been found dead in his home the day before. His niece had been worried when he missed their monthly lunch date and didn't answer his phone when she called, so she went to his house to check on him. His name wasn't released, and an autopsy was pending. Christie was grateful that the flower bouquet wasn't mentioned, although she couldn't be certain that this was the same man Chief mentioned. Shivers ran down her spine anyway. How often would two different men in the same small town die on the same day?

"You think this is the same gentleman who got our flowers, don't you?" Christie asked as she took the paper back to her aunt.

Doris nodded grimly. "I wouldn't be surprised. I hope it wasn't one of our regular customers. That would make me feel even worse than I already do."

Christie put an arm around her aunt's shoulders. "You know we didn't do anything wrong. I'm sure the sheriff's office will figure out what really happened."

Doris sniffled and shrugged off Christie's arm. "I better get back to work on these flowers. I promised this arrangement would be ready by ten for Mrs. Princeton to pick up. She's taking it to her son's office for some kind of special function."

"Would that be Jason Princeton's mother? He and I graduated together."

"Yes, it is. She told me he opened a law office here a few years ago. He got tired of the big city life and ended up here in White Castle."

Christie smiled. "Like me. I wonder if I'll run into him around town."

"Or you could need some legal advice and call on him at his office," suggested her aunt.

"Legal advice? I can't imagine what for." She saw her aunt glance at the newspaper. "Oh, Aunt Doris, don't be silly. I told you we aren't involved in that at all. True, Chief frightened me a bit yesterday, but I know he was just following leads to find a murderer, not really trying to intimidate me."

"Well, that aside, it wouldn't hurt you to meet some of the younger men in town. You could deliver this bouquet yourself and save Mrs. Princeton a trip. And see Jason for yourself." Doris had a sly smile on her face.

"Or I could catch up on these invoices and receipts and stay current with my business ledger. I have to remind myself that

I'm working for myself now, and the bottom line matters. When I worked for the furniture chain, it seemed like I was working with play money. The dollars were just numbers on a screen. Now it's real."

CHRISTIE SAT down at her desk and began working on her electronic accounting system. She found herself wondering if Jason was still as shy as he'd been in high school. She had been the short, bouncy cheerleader who was happy with a B average, while he had been a tall, lean and nerdy straight-A student who took extra math classes and was on the debate and knowledge bowl teams.

The door chime interrupted her reverie. She looked up to see a lovely woman in her sixties walk in. She wore a suit with dress heels and looked as though she worked in some kind of professional office.

"How can I help you?" asked Christie.

"I'm here to pick up some flowers for Princeton," she replied. She had a friendly smile. "I called earlier."

Aunt Doris went to the flower cooler and picked up the bouquet she'd prepared. She placed the vase on the counter, saying, "Here you are, Mrs. Princeton."

"Those are gorgeous! I could never put something like this together," she said. Turning to Christie, she asked, "How much do I owe you?"

"Forty-five dollars plus tax. Shall I put that on your credit card?"

Mrs. Princeton handed over her Visa. "You look very familiar. Are you Maude's granddaughter who used to work here on weekends?"

Christie blushed. "Yes, I'm Christie O'Mara. Your son Jason and I were in the same class. He was our valedictorian. I was an also-ran in the smarts department." Christie finished the transaction and then busied herself with preparing the bouquet for transportation in a cardboard container that she stuffed with wads of newspaper to keep the vase upright.

"It's delightful that you came back to White Castle. So many of our young people go off to bigger cities and never look back."

"Yes, ma'am. I went to San Francisco myself and didn't think about coming back until my grandma died. The flower shop seemed to be calling my name. So far, I'm glad I made the move."

"Well, I will tell Jason that I ran into you." She slung her Kate Spade purse over her shoulder and picked up the box with its flowers. "Perhaps you two once-big-city-returning-home kids will get together since you have that in common." She winked and headed for the door which Doris was holding open for her.

Christie continued entering data into her computer. Maybe it would be nice to see Jason, she mused. But he might very well have a girlfriend already. She sighed and printed the orders for the corsages and boutonnieres that she and Doris would make the next day for the big Saturday night dance at the high school. She checked her floral stock to see if she needed to order a few stems.

She looked up when the door chimed again, and she saw Chief Conway walking toward her desk.

"Hello, Chief Conway. How can I help you?" She tried to sound casual. Maybe he was just there to order flowers?

"Good afternoon, Ms. O'Mara," said the officer. "I'm sorry to have to bother you again, but I have a few questions for you and your Aunt Doris about the man who ordered the flowers that were found at the scene with the dead gentleman."

"Yes, Chief. Go ahead." Okay, so not to order flowers.

Christie's palms felt hot and sweaty. Aunt Doris heard her name and emerged from the flower room.

"Ma'am." Conway tilted his head toward Aunt Doris. "You said you took the order. Did you recognize the voice?"

"No, I did not," Aunt Doris replied. "I've lived here a lot of years, and I'm sure I would have remembered that voice."

"What was it like?" Conway's pen hovered over his notebook. "Can you describe it?"

She lowered her head and thought for a moment. "It was a very low voice. Like a bass singer in a choir. And raspy."

"Do you think you would recognize it if you heard it again?"

"Oh, yes. He sounded sinister." Doris shuddered. "I'm sure I wouldn't want to meet him in a dark alley."

"What about phone records? Did he give you his number?"

Christie opened the log book and found the order for the flowers. "There's no phone number recorded." She looked at her aunt. "Aunt Doris, do you recall why you didn't write it down?"

Doris scoffed. "He said I didn't need it because he was sending someone to pick up the bouquet in person. And when I said it might be helpful in case I had any questions, he hung up on me."

Christie asked Conway, "Can you find the number by checking our phone records? The call came in at two forty that afternoon, according to my aunt's note."

"We can try, but that would take time. It's not like in those television programs where they can get information instantaneously."

"Were you able to track down the license plate from the numbers that I gave to you?"

Conway smiled grimly. "There are over a thousand cars in the western half of the state with those numbers, and at least twenty of them are BMWs. So, no help for the moment."

Christie scrunched her face and put her hands on her hips. "And that was my best lead." She thought for a moment, then asked, "Are you able to narrow it down by color?"

"Probably not by much. BMW owners tend to like black, it appears." Conway gave her another of his quizzical looks, then pocketed his notebook and pen. "That's all I need for today. Thank you for your time."

Once he was out the door, Christie said to her aunt. "I don't like the idea of a murderer on the loose in White Castle. Especially one using my shop as a well, I don't know — message center, I guess."

"Well, not for long, I'd hope. At least they are working to solve it. I'm hoping they arrest someone soon."

"Hmm." Christie scrunched her face in thought. "Arresting someone soon was what they did in Arnold Youngman's death forty years ago. That news article that I read at the library said they had another suspect, but he left town. By convicting a man, they solved the case — at least in the district attorney's eyes. Maybe they solved it by convicting the wrong guy all too soon."

Her aunt gave a little shudder. "If they didn't catch the other man, it could mean there are still *two* murderers on the loose."

Christie shrugged. "He's probably dead by now anyway."

Aunt Doris shook her head. "If he was in his twenties or thirties then, he'd only be in his sixties or seventies now. That's not that old these days and hardly means he's dead." She sniffed, and Christie realized her elderly aunt's idea of age was far different from her own.

"You're right, of course. I hadn't thought of it that way. There *could* be two murderers out there somewhere," said

Christie. "Because I can't imagine there is a connection between the murders. Whoever the suspect was all those years ago would probably have stayed away."

Her aunt smiled and said, "We don't know for sure that he ever left, just that he wasn't found at the time."

Christie, once again, saw that mischievous and secretive look in her aunt's stoic face. "You think he's still around, don't you? Do you know who they thought it was at the time?"

Aunt Doris raised an eyebrow and turned to go back to her worktable, where another order for a bouquet of flowers waited for her.

TWELVE

Christie went back to the library after taking Stormy home. It was too cold outside to leave the kitty in the car while she scrolled through the newspapers looking for follow-up reports on Arnold Youngman. She read through the weekly *White Castle Gazette* issues for the two months following the murder trial. The only article she found was a brief mention that there had been no further leads in the case.

She asked the librarian for the microfiche files for the larger newspaper in Granite City, which was fifteen miles down the freeway. Being a larger city, it was a daily paper. Christie soon discovered that coverage of White Castle news events was sparse. She did, however, find a mention of the investigating officer's name: Dwight H. Smith. She recalled that Jack Smith, the neighbor, had mentioned that his father had been a deputy sheriff at the time. Did Jack know more than he was telling?

~

CHRISTIE BOUNCED into her shop Friday morning, ready to help her aunt create the boutonnieres and corsages for the high school dance that evening. She laughed when she saw Aunt Doris dressed in a witch costume, black pointed hat and all. She had draped a string of orange lights shaped like pumpkins around her neck and wore black cat earrings. Doris did a pirouette to show off her outfit, then handed a plastic bag to Christie.

"Here's your costume. Maude and I always dressed up for Halloween. Your customers will love it, especially the young people who will be picking up these orders." She winked at her niece as Christie peeked into the bag.

"Cinderella? You want me to dress up as Cinderella?" Christie held up the blue and white dress. "I'm not anything like a princess."

"Are you implying that my costume says something about me?" Doris wrapped florist tape around the stems of the purple and white carnations which would be pinned onto a young man's lapel.

"No, of course not. I didn't mean it that way." Christie stared at the dress. "I've just never been the Cinderella type."

"Well, for today, you will be. Your blonde hair is why I chose this outfit. You'll look perfect without having to wear a wig. And you're welcome."

Christie smiled at her aunt. "Thank you, Aunt Doris. That's sweet of you. You're right. It will be fun to be dressed up, considering it's Halloween."

A few minutes later, after changing in the small restroom, "Cinderella" joined the Wicked Witch. "Let the day begin," Christie announced as she unlocked the front door.

The two women had finished most of the orders by the time the first of the local teens came through the door during their lunch hour from school.

"Cool!" and "Nice get-ups" were the most common comments from the customers as Christie rang up their purchases.

The shop was quiet during the early afternoon except for the sporadic customer who came in to browse for a gift or card. Christie assumed most of the local townspeople were busy readying for the onslaught of trick-or-treaters who would be ringing doorbells at their homes once it got dark. She was at her back desk entering the day's transactions into the electronic ledger when the phone at the front counter rang.

"Will you get that, please?" her aunt called from the storage room. "I'm busy back here."

"Christie's Flower Shoppe," said Christie. "How can I help you?"

Christie caught her breath when a deep and raspy voice replied, "I'd like to place an order, please." She noted the time.

"Certainly. What would you like?"

The raspy voice requested an arrangement of flowers to be picked up the next morning. "I want yellow chrysanthemums and at least one orange lily. Do you have those in stock?"

"I'll check. One minute, please." Christie carried the handset to the flower room and confirmed she had the blooms. "I do. Do you have any other specific requests?"

"You can use anything else that goes with the mums and lilies."

"Is there a message you'd like on the card?"

"That's not necessary."

"Okay. May I have your name and a phone number?"

"Mr. Jones will pick them up tomorrow about ten. You won't need to call him."

"But I need a number in case—"

The dial tone sounded in her ear. Christie stared at the

handset as if it had more information, then went back to the flower room.

"Aunt Doris, I just got another order from the raspy-voiced man."

"What kind of message did he want this time?"

"He asked for yellow mums and an orange lily. I haven't looked up their meanings yet, but I bet they stand for something."

Aunt Doris said seriously, "The yellow mums convey the message that someone feels slighted, and an orange lily is supposed to signify revenge. What other flowers did he mention?"

"Those are the only ones he specified. He said I could use whatever else I wanted. He wouldn't give me his name or a number, just like with you."

"Are you going to call the sheriff's office?" Aunt Doris walked back to the flower room.

"And do what? Report another strange order? It's not a crime, I suppose. But he might want to know about it in case it helps him identify the BMW."

"Maybe you could sneak a photo of the guy who picks them up," suggested Aunt Doris.

"And how would I do that?"

"This is when a security camera could be helpful. Or I could take a picture from the back of the shop while you take care of the order."

"Or I could take a picture of the car when he leaves since you won't be here when he said they're to be picked up."

"I like that idea for now, but I still think setting up a surveillance system is a good plan overall."

"You're right, Auntie. I'll ask Anita to help me with that. I can invite her down to the shop on Saturday when she's done with teaching. I want to spiff up the gift section, and she's got a designer's eye."

CHRISTIE CALLED the Chief about her plan. He was okay with her taking a picture of the car when Mr. Jones picked up the flowers, and supported her plan to install a surveillance system. He cautioned her to be careful and circumspect, however.

CHAPTER

THIRTEEN

Christie had decided to participate in a holiday promotion organized by the local downtowners' association to hand out Halloween candy between four and six p.m. The organizers hoped the event would attract potential customers who would check out the shopping opportunities right in their hometown while their children filled their bags with treats. She wasn't sure it would help her own business much, but she remembered how much she loved going door-to-door as a kid. For the children who lived in the country where houses were farther apart, trick-or-treating downtown was a popular option.

Christie and Doris happily handed out the fun-size bars of Almond Joys, KitKats and Reese's Peanut Butter Cups to the costumed children. It was almost six fifteen before Christie was able to lock the glass door and flip the "Open" sign to "Closed."

"I'm sure glad I bought the giant-sized bags of candy bars for this," said Christie. "I was sure I had too many treats, but I didn't want to run out early."

"I'd call that a success," said Aunt Doris. "I saw a lot of unfamiliar faces. Maybe we'll get some new customers."

"Maybe. It was good for public relations, if nothing else. I'll hand out these last few treats to customers tomorrow until they're gone. Thanks for the help. I'll see you Monday."

After her aunt had gone Christie glanced around the store before reaching behind her desk to turn off the interior lights. She was more than ready to call it a day. She caught a glimpse out of the corner of her eye of movement at the front door and jumped. It took a moment to register that a man was poised to knock. Another moment later, she walked briskly to the door and opened it for Jason Princeton.

"Jason! What a surprise to see you here!" Christie stepped aside, looking up at him as she let him in and relocked the door.

"Hi, Christie. I wasn't sure how to find you except here at your store. My mom told me you had reopened it after your grandma passed. And I wanted to tell you the flowers my mom picked up for the office were beautiful." Jason stood with his hands in his front pockets, shifting his lanky form from foot to foot.

"That's so sweet of you."

Jason nodded, his face reddening as he glanced quickly at her, up and down. "Is that a princess dress you're wearing?"

Christie looked at her attire and laughed, having forgotten she was in costume. "Yes, I've been Cinderella all day, thanks to Aunt Doris. I hear you're an attorney now. So, how's work going here? Are you busy enough in a small town like this?"

"That's kind of why I stopped by. I was hoping you could go out for a drink and chat a bit. I can tell you about it. Mom said you'd settled back home from the big city, and I thought, well..."

"I'd love to. When?"

He blinked. "Oh. Are you free tonight? We could get dinner, too, if you like."

"I don't have anything going on. And that sounds lovely," said Christie as she bent over to pick up the cat who had brushed against her leg. "This is Stormy. She's my shop cat. Aunt Doris said my grandma used to feed her on the back step. I decided to adopt her. She keeps me company here and at home."

Jason reached out to pet the cat. Stormy stretched her head up to meet his hand and purred loudly.

"She likes you," said Christie, pleasantly amused. "She seems to be a pretty good judge of character. I need to take her home to feed her and change my clothes. I'd feel a little silly showing up as Cinderella. Although, I suppose on Halloween it wouldn't be totally inappropriate." They both laughed. "I can meet you somewhere in about a half hour if that's okay with you."

"Sure thing. The White Castle Grill has pretty good food and a decent atmosphere. Do you know where that is?"

"I do. Mom and I had lunch there a couple of weeks ago."

"Great. I'll see you there, say, about seven?"

"I'll be there."

After he left, Christie snuggled Stormy for another moment before putting her in the carrier. *Does my cat really know good guys from bad guys?* she wondered as she locked up the business.

CHRISTIE PERUSED HER CLOSET. She didn't want to dress up too much, thinking it might send the wrong message. But she wanted to dress differently from her normal work clothes. She finally settled on charcoal bootcut jeans with a burgundy turtleneck sweater, a jeans jacket and black boots. Smiling at her image in the mirror, she added a touch of glossy lipstick and an extra flick of mascara. *I'm acting like it's a date,* she thought to herself and shrugged.

Jason had secured a table near the front window at the restaurant. He smiled and waved at her and stood up as she approached. He helped her with her coat and chair. "You look nice," he said once he sat down. "Would you like to order something to drink?"

"That would be perfect. I would love a glass of merlot," said Christie, glancing around the room to see if she knew anyone. She recognized a couple of her parents' friends and the faces of one or two customers who shopped at the store.

"Thank you for saying you'd join me for dinner," said Jason as he signaled the waiter. "It beats eating alone on a Friday night. I don't know many people in town except my staff, my family and clients."

"What about our classmates? A few of them are around, I've noticed."

"In case you don't remember, I wasn't exactly 'Mr. Popularity' back then." Jason paused to give the waiter their drinks order.

Christie grinned when he ordered two glasses of merlot. "I figured you for a martini kind of guy, being an attorney and all."

Jason reddened. "I prefer a nice wine to those stiff drinks my fellow attorneys were drinking in my first law group."

"Where were you working? I don't think your mom mentioned that when she came by."

"Seattle, but I didn't like the size of the city or the commute. I guess I'm a small-town guy, after all. And the pressure of being an associate doing all the grunt work for the partners was more than I wanted." He paused when the waiter approached with the two glasses. "So, I left as soon as I had fulfilled my five-year agreement and came here."

"Sounds like something worth toasting," said Christie, raising her glass. "Here's to small towns."

"Agreed," said Jason, raising his glass as well before taking a sip. "This is pretty good for a house wine. Mom and Dad eat here frequently and recommended it."

"Good choice all around, so far. I recall Mr. Thompson was the local attorney most people used back then. Are you in with him, or did you buy his practice?"

"I sort of bought it. He wanted to retire and practically gave it to me when he found out I was planning to start work here. He offered to stay on for a few weeks to help me get started and wouldn't accept payment for anything except one month's rent when I opened for business. He owns the building and has a couple of other renters. He said he was happy to have someone young take over and take care of his longtime clients. So far, it's worked out well."

Christie and Jason quickly perused the menu when they saw the waiter come back toward the table with his order pad in hand.

"I guess it's not going to be like it is in France, where we chat for a half hour before we order a meal," said Christie after the waiter left with their orders. "I spent a month abroad and never got used to their three-hour meals."

"Are you a dine-and-dash kind of girl?" Jason teased.

"Only when I'm going to be late to the store to open up in the morning. Fortunately, Aunt Doris is always on time and usually opens up for me."

"I remember your Aunt Doris. She somehow remembered all of our names when we came to pick up corsages for the dances. I thought she was great."

"That she is. I couldn't manage without her. She knows

everyone!" Christie rolled her eyes. "Except she didn't know the man who ordered a strange bouquet last week."

"Strange? How?"

Christie related a short version of the story about the man with the raspy voice and the message he wanted to convey with flowers. "I was more than upset when Chief Conway came to tell me that the person who got the bouquet was found dead the next day. I'm not sure he believed me that none of the flowers were actually deadly."

"Do you know how he died?"

"Not for sure, but hopefully, it was a heart attack or something natural like that."

"Well, if you need an attorney, I'll be happy to help."

Their beef tenderloin and chicken marsala were hot and delicious when they arrived a little later. Jason ordered more wine to go with their meals.

"Your family has been around here for a long time, right?" asked Christie between mouthfuls.

Jason nodded. "My grandparents came here from Nebraska in the fifties when grandfather needed work. He'd heard there were good jobs in the mills in the area. Why?"

"Do you know the name Arnold Youngman or Teresa Stewart?"

Jason tilted his head and furrowed his brow. "No, I don't think so. Why?"

Christie told him about the desk and how she came up with the names. "I can't explain why I want to figure out who they were except for the letter in the desk. It's like a little mystery that fell into my lap."

"But this all happened years ago. Statute of limitations would probably play a role even if you did find out who they were and where they are now."

Christie said playfully, "Spoilsport. Will you at least ask your mom if she remembers them? Please?"

"Of course, with one condition."

"And that is...?"

"You agree to have dinner with me next week so I can tell you the answer."

CHAPTER
FOURTEEN

Christie found herself smiling while she changed into comfy clothes after her dinner date. She looked forward to a second date when he might have some information for her.

Stormy purred in her lap and batted at the yarn, which made it difficult to knit the hats she'd decided to make for the community project, "Hats for the Homeless." Instead, she scrolled through the options on her television and settled on the Hallmark Channel. The movies were always squeaky-clean and heartwarming, which is what she wanted at the moment.

Before long, her mind wandered back to the mystery of Missy and B of the letter from the desk. And to the death of the mystery man who had received the flowers from her shop. His identity still hadn't been released, supposedly because the next of kin hadn't been notified. Christie found that very puzzling. *Whom can I call that might know the identity of the victim?* she asked herself. She wished she knew someone who worked at the hospital or as an EMT. Realizing that she didn't personally know anyone who qualified, she called her mom, who volunteered at the hospital on a regular basis.

"Hi, Honey. What's on your mind?"

"Hey. Did you have a slug of trick-or-treaters at your house?"

"The usual number, about a hundred kids. What about at the shop? I bet you had a mob down there."

"That we did! I bought two giant bags of mini-sized candy bars, and we gave out almost every single one of them."

"Aunt Doris told me she talked you into wearing a costume. I almost came down to see that," said Maureen, chuckling.

"I was the reluctant Cinderella waiting for the handsome prince," said Christie. She found herself blushing, glad her mother couldn't see it, when she thought of Jason coming by while she was still in costume.

"So why did you call? I doubt it was about Halloween."

Christie told her mom about the man who had died and that her shop card had been found at his house. And about the raspy-voiced man. "What I really want to know is if you know someone who might have inside information, like who was the guy that died."

"I hadn't heard about it yet, but I could ask around at the hospital tomorrow. I have a shift in the morning at the main desk. One of the other volunteers, Liz, always seems to know everything that goes on."

"That'd be great! Thanks, Mom."

"How are you otherwise, Christie? Are you happy at the shop?"

"Way happier than I was in San Francisco. I like being in charge of my future, whatever it turns out to be. I even went out on kind of a date with Jason Princeton. He treated me to dinner at the White Castle Grill earlier this evening. And asked me to go out again in a week."

"That's nice. He was in your class, wasn't he? His mother and I aren't great friends, but we run into each other now and then. She's always seemed very cordial."

"Jason promised to ask his mom if she knew Arnold Youngman, the guy who died forty years ago, or Teresa Stewart, who might be the mysterious Missy."

"You're still trying to figure that out? That's truly ancient history, Honey. And you're not a detective. Besides, the murder has been solved, and for all you know, Missy and B found each other, got married, and lived happily ever after."

Christie bristled. "I'm just curious about that letter I found in the desk. It reminds me of some of the Nancy Drew mysteries I read as a kid."

"Those were fiction, Christie. Not true stories."

"Maybe so, but it doesn't hurt to do a little researching."

Christie felt exasperated after her conversation. She sensed her mother was right about the letter, but she wasn't ready to give up her sleuthing. She called Anita as she had promised her aunt.

Christie gave Anita a *CliffsNotes* version of the unusual floral arrangement orders. She said, "It's probably not necessary, but I hope I can get a photo of the man who picks up the flowers for the so-called Mr. Jones."

"That doesn't sound too dangerous, Christie. I'm free all morning if you need me."

"And I could also use your discerning eye to help me with improving the set-ups around the shop. I'm good with numbers but not so much with how to make things attractive. You were always very creative in school."

"Thanks for the compliment. Playing 'interior designer'

will be a nice break from grading essay papers about fifteenth century English literature."

"I can pay you, but it'll be minimum wage."

Anita laughed. "It'll be my treat to help you. You can buy me lunch instead."

"It's a deal. I close at noon on Saturdays, so we can have lunch with a grown-up beverage at the White Castle Grill if you like."

CHAPTER
FIFTEEN

The morning was crisp and clear, albeit chilly at thirty-five degrees, when Christie arrived at the shop Saturday morning. She quickly surveyed the displays and picked up a few stray items that belonged elsewhere as she walked to the front to open for business. She'd asked Anita to come in at nine thirty, which she thought would give her enough time to set up a camera to catch Mr. Jones on film.

Christie hummed along with the background music, a favorite CD of classical music, while she filled an amber-colored vase with yellow mums, white daisies, a couple of orange lilies, and a few stems of purple statice. She tucked in greenery of eucalyptus and myrtle leaves to finish the arrangement. She smiled as she admired her work, then frowned when she found herself thinking of the raspy voice. "I hope you aren't killer flowers," she said aloud, hands on her hips.

She jumped when she heard the chime sound at the front door. It was Anita, right on time, carrying a small tote bag.

"Hi, Anita. I'm in the back arranging flowers." Christie dried her hands and waved, then walked up to meet her friend.

"How about setting your gear here on the counter while I explain what I'm thinking?"

Christie walked Anita through the flower pick-up process and let Anita decide the best position for setting up a surveillance camera.

"I found these at the electronics store. The clerk explained how to use them and made it sound really easy."

"Great. I'll reimburse you, of course. If they work, I can leave them in position and use them on a regular basis."

"That's what I was thinking. Even small businesses are at risk these days, maybe more so than the big stores."

Christie took care of several gift item sales while Anita went to work installing the devices. Stormy supervised from her elevated perch, occasionally hopping down for a scratch behind her ears from Christie or Anita. She wasn't picky.

Anita and Christie tested the angles to find the best position for the main camera. Shortly before ten, they finished the trials and declared the system ready to go. Anita then meandered around the shop, critically analyzing the displays as a designer and as a shopper.

Christie busied herself with making a list of the flowers her aunt would order on Monday, keeping an eye on the front door. She also perused the online florists' displays for ideas for her own arrangements. She was particularly drawn to the ikebana style and sketched out a few simple designs that she would try when she had the opportunity.

It was almost eleven o'clock before a lone gentleman entered the shop. Mr. Jones wore a black winter coat over charcoal slacks and a gray turtleneck sweater, with a black watch plaid scarf and black fedora. He paused and furtively cast an eye in all directions before venturing closer toward Christie, who was sitting at the counter.

She smiled and hoped her racing heart wasn't obvious to him. "How can I help you, sir?"

He looked behind Christie, then glanced at Anita, who had moved closer to the front window. "Do you have an order for Mr. Jones?" he asked quietly. No raspy voice.

"Yes, sir. Just a moment, and I'll get it from the cooler for you." Christie walked to the flower room, opened the cooler door, and retrieved the eye-catching bouquet. After placing it in a sturdy box for travel, she paused at the doorway and picked up a pencil. She wrote a quick note and handed it to Anita, then surreptitiously pressed the "record" button on the surveillance system's remote. She was careful to stay clear of the camera's eye when she returned to the counter with the flowers. Stormy had jumped down from her throne and was standing on the counter looking at Mr. Jones, her back arched, hair standing on end.

"Here you are, Mr. Jones. That'll be fifty-nine dollars and thirty-nine cents including tax. Will that be cash or card today?"

The gentleman handed her three twenty-dollar bills. "Keep the change. Thanks."

"I'll put the coins into this donation jar for the local humane society," she said, pointing to the glass container with a picture of sad-looking dogs. "Thank you, and have a good day."

Anita waited a couple of minutes after the man had driven away in a late-model Acura, then hurried to confer with Christie. "I got the license plate number, as you asked. Did you recognize him?"

Christie nodded. "It's not the same car as last time, but it's the same man. I managed to record him, and I'll call the sheriff's office to let Conway know."

Stormy sat on the counter, her tail flicking back and forth. "I don't think my cat liked him. That's her 'angry' tail."

"Let's check the recording before you call the sheriff to be sure it worked."

Christie squealed when she saw the images scroll by. Stormy's cameo appearance confirmed her displeasure with the man.

"It worked," said Anita. "Now you can call Chief Conway."

CHAPTER

SIXTEEN

Christie waited until noon, when she was ready to close the shop, to call Conway. She didn't want to alarm potential customers if he decided to arrive to talk to her in person while shoppers were present.

"Go ahead and flip the 'Open' sign to 'Closed,'" she called out to Anita, who had decided to stay to keep Christie company. "Conway said he'd come to the back door so you can lock the door as well. Here, catch." She tossed the keys as easily as she used to throw a softball.

Once the door was secured, Christie dimmed the lights of the store except for the lights in the flower room and over her desk. She'd watched a video suggested by her insurance agent and learned a number of useful tips for small business owners. Even though she was expecting a visitor, she jumped when she heard a loud knock at the back door. Stormy sat up and made a low-pitched, growly sound.

She peeked through the tiny window in the door and let out her breath when she saw Chief Conway's face.

"Thank you for coming by, Chief," said Christie. "I have a

video of the man who picked up the second phone order from the man with the raspy voice." She played it through to the end. Stormy jumped down to the counter and walked toward the policeman.

Conway replayed it, watching the video with narrowed eyes.

"I swear I've seen this man before, but I can't tell you where," he said after the second viewing. "Did you notice anything else about him?"

"He's the same gentleman that picked up the first bouquet, but it wasn't the same car. My friend Anita got his license plate number. She's the one who set up the video cameras for me." Christie gave the officer the slip of paper. Anita had also noted that the car was a late-model Acura sedan in charcoal gray.

"What about the flowers? Did the man ordering the flowers specify a message this time?"

"Yes, and no. He asked for yellow chrysanthemums, which can mean someone feels slighted, and orange lilies, which signify revenge."

"Did he tell you that was his message?"

"No, but he specifically selected those flowers. He then said I could use anything else that I wanted and that a Mr. Jones would pick them up Saturday morning. He had a raspy voice like Aunt Doris described for the earlier order."

"Okay. Anything else? Was there anyone else in the car?"

Anita answered, "No, sir. He was alone."

"Did you see which direction he went?"

"I watched him until he turned right at the stoplight. From there, he could have gone onto the freeway in either direction or straight along the overpass into the main part of town. I couldn't see that far from the store."

"Well, thank you, ladies. I'll put out an APB and see if

anyone spots this car, especially if he's gone on the freeway or to a neighboring town."

"Good luck," said Christie. "I hope you catch the guy. It's creepy to think my grandma's shop could be involved in anything like murder."

Conway half-smiled. "I guess I can tell you that the man who died earlier had a heart attack. It wasn't your killer flowers, after all. So you can stop worrying that his death might be your fault."

Christie sighed a big breath of relief. "Thank goodness. That makes me feel a little better. Is there anything else you can tell me?"

"Not just yet. We're still trying to figure out if there's anything else in the victim's background that's related to the messages of the flowers. Have a good day." He touched his fingers to the brim of his hat and left through the back door.

Anita fiddled with the makeshift security camera for a moment while Christie wiped off the counters. "I can set up something more sophisticated to beef up your ADT monitoring system for you, Christie. It would be a safety feature that I think you need, and it won't be expensive at all." She mentally sized up the shop. "A couple of cameras inside, front and back, and motion sensor detection lights at the back door should do it. What do you think?"

Christie nodded slowly, eyebrows furrowed. "I like that idea. You can hook it up to my laptop or cell, can't you?"

"Yes, absolutely. And to ADT as well. I'll get all the materials today, and we can hook it up as soon as tomorrow if you wish."

"Sounds good, but how do you know how to do something like that?"

Anita shrugged. "I dated a security guy for a while when I lived in Seattle. He insisted on setting up my apartment. Turns out it's pretty easy. Even an anthropologist-turned-school teacher can do it."

"And it might be handy if you ever want to do theatre work around here."

Anita smiled and executed a dramatic stage bow before joining Christie in a big laugh.

CHAPTER

SEVENTEEN

Anita showed up at the shop Sunday afternoon carrying a carton filled with a variety of small boxes. Christie peeked in and saw cameras, motion detector lights and the miscellany required to install said items.

"You'll have to tell me what to do to help you," said Christie. "I'm good with computers once they're ready to use, but not the setting-up part."

"You can help by standing in different areas of the store while I figure out the best locations for the cameras. I want to cover as much square footage as possible with the three cameras. I only bought one sensor light for the back. I figured most bad people would try entering from that side instead of the front. The store is pretty well-lit at night from the front, I've noticed."

"Okay. That makes sense."

Christie moved from spot to spot as instructed until Anita was satisfied with the location of the camera at the front of the store. Christie held the ladder while Anita installed the device near the ceiling. While Anita checked the monitor, Christie pretended to be shopping, adding some acting comedy to her role. Even Stormy got into the act, having jumped down from her shelf. She sat next to Anita and watched her owner on the monitor.

"I wonder what she's thinking," said Anita. "She's probably never seen two of you at once before."

"Maybe she thinks she'll get two dinners with two of me," said Christie, chuckling.

Christie and Anita repeated the process for the other two cameras, placing one in a position to monitor the area around the sales desk and the third one closest to the back door, where the camera could also see the flower cooler and workroom.

Finally, they installed the security light directly over the back door, but high enough that someone couldn't simply reach up to unscrew the bulb. Anita cited her friend telling her of an experience like that happening to one of his clients. After coaching Christie on how to arm and disarm the cameras and having her do it herself a couple of times, Anita pronounced her an expert.

"Anita, you're a gem. I couldn't have done this on my own. Let me treat you to dinner."

"Works for me. I'm super hungry after all this critical thinking."

"See you at Plaza Jalisco in fifteen minutes."

"Margaritas and enchiladas, a perfect combination," said Christie. "I'm in food heaven."

"This arroz con pollo is pretty awesome as well." Anita followed a bite of the chicken with rice with a swallow of her drink. "I have never understood why my version of this at home is never as good. What's the secret?"

"I think it must be the special sauces or something. But I don't mind because this way I always have an excuse for going out to eat. It tastes better!"

Anita and Christie saluted their waiter, Larry, who stopped at their table and asked if everything was okay.

"It's always good," said Christie. "Compliments to the chef." Christie knew the chef was Larry's dad, who owned the business.

"Have you heard any more from the sheriff about the man who died?" asked Anita.

Christie shook her head and said, "Not yet, except he died from a heart attack. My mom promised to ask around at the hospital the next time she was doing her volunteer thing. She said it seems like some of them always know what's going on and that one of the leaders works three shifts a week."

"She probably knows as much as anyone. If she staffs the information desk, she would have access to the names of patients."

"They always have a couple of staff near the emergency department entrance as well because that's the way many visitors enter the hospital."

"Will you let me know when you find out?"

"Sure. Oh, I just thought of something." Christie pulled out her phone and scrolled to the picture from the yearbook. "I totally forgot to show you this photo earlier. Is this the Lynette you were thinking of?"

"Yes, I'm sure of it. Do you think this is the same person you saw at the store?"

Christie sighed. "I want it to be, but I'm not convinced. She seemed more than four years older than we are. More like ten or more."

"Maybe she's had a rough life. Or she smokes. Or something."

"Or any or all of the above. Even if she is the same person, we still have to track her down. Then I'd know."

"Did you say 'we' have to track her down?" Anita raised an eyebrow. "You're the one with the mystery, not me."

"But you're helping, aren't you?"

"I said I'd ask around at the high school, but I don't know what else I can do."

"That's good for starters."

CHAPTER

EIGHTEEN

Christie dunked her toe into the water and was pleasantly surprised to find that it was warmer than she expected. She walked, step by step, deeper into the ocean until the water was chest-high. She closed her eyes and let her body float to the surface under the bright afternoon sun. *This is heaven,* she thought.

In the distance, she heard a clanging sound. She tuned it out and let the azure-blue, Caribbean water envelop her. The clanging sound changed to a telephone ring. *That's odd. How could I hear a telephone out here when my cell phone is on the beach?* The ringing was incessant.

She stood up in the water and looked around. She shook her head and opened her eyes again. Her phone was ringing on the nightstand, and she was wrapped not in tropical water but in her warm comforter. She grabbed the phone.

"Hello?"

"Ms. O'Mara, this is Mikayla at ADT, your security company. I'm calling to let you know that the alarm at your business has been triggered. I've already alerted the police."

Christie noted the time on her bedside clock. Two twenty a.m. "Thank you. I'll go right down."

She dressed in record time, grabbed her keys and raced the mile or so to her flower shop. A police car was there, parked in front, lights flashing. Christie jumped out and hurried to the officer standing at the door.

"Hi, officer. I'm Christie O'Mara. This is my business. What can you tell me?" She glanced at his name tag, which read L. Samuels.

"Yes, Miss. The back door was broken to gain entrance. No one is inside. You can go in now. I'll go in with you if you like."

"Yes, I'd like that."

Officer Samuels and Christie drove around to the back door, where a second officer was keeping watch. Christie let out an involuntary wail when she saw the broken glass of the door's window. She opened the door slowly, afraid of what she would find. She flicked on the light switch and disarmed the alarm.

Her heart sank when she saw the tubs of flowers emptied, water all over the floor. "No, no, no!" she sobbed.

"I'm sorry, Miss O'Mara. I know this is a mess, but can you walk around and tell me if anything is missing?"

Christie nodded, tears abating, and walked around her store. Her file drawers had been dumped on the floor. "It will be impossible to tell for sure if anything was missing until I put them back in place," she said. Her eyes wandered through the displays, seeing nothing out of order until she glanced at the empty space where the writing desk had stood earlier that day.

"The vintage writing desk is gone." She gasped and covered her mouth with her hand. "And it appears to be the only thing missing. I wonder if it's because of the letter."

"I'm not following you."

Christie related the story about the letter that she had

found in the desk and how she had been doing some research to try to figure out if it pertained to something real or not.

"Have you talked with Chief Conway about this? He hasn't shared this with the others on staff."

"Not exactly, but he's been here because of a recent death of someone who received flowers from my shop earlier last week."

Officer Samuels smiled. "Oh, yes. The killer flowers."

"My flowers did not kill the man, whoever he was." Christie narrowed her eyes at the officer.

Samuels' grin disappeared. "I'm sorry, Miss. That just slipped out. The name of the man you're talking about was Jerry Ferguson. He apparently died of a heart attack. But your flowers were there on his table."

"I understand that's why the police chief came by. But that's the first time I've heard the man's name. Is the cause of his death now official?"

"Yes, Miss. His niece had been trying to contact him and found him on the floor. The EMTs tried CPR, but he was already gone. They pronounced him dead on arrival at the hospital. And an autopsy verified the cause."

"Thank you for telling me."

"One of the daytime officers will come to see you tomorrow and check your security videos. I see that you have a couple of cameras, and hopefully, your system was turned on."

Christie said with a weak smile, "My friend and I installed it just today. Maybe we got lucky, and we'll see who was here."

"Miss O'Mara, I think you should tell Chief Conway about the desk and the letter now that this has happened. You may have stirred up a hornet's nest."

Christie nodded with a grim smile on her face, Jack Smith's comment about letting a sleeping dog lie having come once again to mind.

CHAPTER

NINETEEN

Christie slept fitfully until her alarm chirped her awake at six thirty. She felt groggy and out of sorts after the night of interrupted and restless sleep. She stumbled around her house, started her coffeemaker and took a quick shower. She felt more alert after her second cup of java.

She called her aunt to warn her of the broken glass and promised to arrive at the shop earlier than usual. She reminded herself to check her home file for the folder with the letter about the desk and B's note to Missy before she left the house.

Despite her intent, Christie didn't beat Aunt Doris to the shop. She heard her aunt mumbling aloud when she entered and quickly hung her coat and purse in the tiny storage closet. She put a smile on her face and sauntered into the main shop area.

"Hi, Aunt Doris. I was trying to get here before you today, but I've failed again."

Her aunt harrumphed. "I'm going to have to order some replacements for the flowers that were damaged last night."

She grumbled under her breath. "Why did they have to make such a mess?"

Christie put an arm around her aunt's shoulders. "I'm sorry you had to come into this. I hoped I would have it all cleaned up before you got here."

Doris shrugged Christie's arm off. "I noticed the desk was gone. I suppose that's what this was all about, don't you think?"

Christie nodded. "Yes, I think so. But even though the desk is gone, I have the Missy note safe at my house. As well as the letter I found from the lady who gave the desk to Grandma."

"I hope you put those in a safe place. If that's what these scallywags were looking for, they might try your house next."

"I thought of that, too. I'm going to ask Jason to keep them safe for now. He was going to do some research for me anyway, so I could kill two birds with one stone."

"What kind of research?" Aunt Doris busied herself with making one of her specialty arrangements, which had been requested for a client's ninetieth birthday.

She had a way of combining unusual items, such as peacock or pheasant feathers, with blooms to create an extraordinarily colorful display. Aunt Doris had become known for her talent in the area. Her customers often requested that she use something special that a loved one had owned, particularly as she was creating funeral flowers. Today, the request had been to incorporate a set of salt and pepper shakers that had been in the family since a visit to Norway many years before.

Christie answered her aunt, "Jason said he would ask his mother if she knew Arnold Youngman. His family has been in the area since the fifties, it seems."

"I thought you already knew that Mr. Youngman was from around here."

"Yes, you told me that. I'm still curious about Missy and B and if the three of them knew each other."

"I'll say it again — that's all in the past. And it doesn't matter anymore."

"Maybe I'm barking up the wrong tree about it, but he offered to ask his mom, and I accepted." Christie grinned. "He wanted me to agree to go to dinner again, and I think this was his way of being sure I'd say yes."

Aunt Doris's eyes widened as she wrinkled her forehead. "He did, did he? Well, you could do worse than to go out with that nice young man." She stuck one last bit of greenery into the vase, then stepped back, her hands on her hips. "Well, what do you think?" The brightly colored Norwegian salt and pepper set had been wired to wooden stakes that were nestled in a bouquet of white, blue and yellow flowers, matching and coordinating with the painted ceramic shakers. The final result resembled a painting of spring flowers.

Christie squealed and clapped her hands. "That's lovely and clever. Mrs. Schneider will love it." She kissed her aunt's pink cheek.

"I'll give her daughter a call and let her know she can pick it up."

Christie was halfway done with the job of replacing the papers in the file drawers when the door chimed to let her know that a visitor had entered. Chief Conway walked in, a grim look on his face.

"Hello, Chief," said Christie. "How can I help you?"

"Good morning, Miss O'Mara. Officer Samuels reported that you might have some security footage from the break-in last night. May I see it?"

"Oh, yes. Let me boot up my laptop and see what it shows."

Christie spent a few seconds searching for the icon that Anita had installed on her desktop screen. "Here it is." She went through the steps to find recordings and found nothing. "Uh oh. I'm not finding anything." She groaned.

"Let me take a crack at it. I do this all the time." Chief Conway whistled a little tune while pressing a series of buttons. "Okay. I found the file listing for all stored recordings." He was quiet for a moment, then he frowned and pronounced, "Nothing." He looked at Christie. "Are you sure you had it set properly when you were done with the installation?"

"I think so. Let me check my notes quickly." Christie found the paper with the instructions from Anita. She read through them, then clapped her head with her hand and said, "Dang. I forgot to hit the 'reset' button like I was supposed to when I left the shop."

Chief Conway nodded and said, "Happens all the time when you get a new system. Let me show you a simple method to help you remember when you leave tonight."

Christie felt her face redden from her bungled attempt as she nodded soberly. "Okay. Thank you."

A few minutes later, Conway finished the instructions, which were similar to Anita's but made more sense to Christie.

"I'm sorry you had to come here for nothing," said Christie. "These guys probably won't come back now that they have the desk."

Conway cocked his head. "Maybe or maybe not. They still might want that note you told me about earlier. I hope it's in a very safe place, young lady."

Christie nodded, her face flushed. "It'll be in an even better place later today. Thank you, Chief. I'll set the system properly from now on."

CHAPTER

TWENTY

Monday appeared to be a slow day in the world of flowers. A handful of browsers popped in during the day, but the main excitement of the afternoon was when Christie's dad arrived shortly after the lunch hour to repair the broken glass in the back door.

"I brought a new lock for you as well, Christie. You have to use a key to open it from the inside as well as the outside, so it'll be tougher for someone to just reach in and open the door. They'd have to crawl in through the window instead, but they'll have to remove the glass and wire first. It'll slow someone down, maybe, just enough to alert the police."

"That sounds great, Dad." Christie hugged him and sneaked a kiss on his cheek. "I so appreciate you fixing the window. Let me know what I owe you for materials."

"This is on me, kid. I want to keep my daughter safe."

While her dad fixed the window, Christie ordered the flowers she wanted to keep on hand for orders that she hoped would come in during the week. She knew from her time working for the furniture store that there were peaks and valleys in sales. The floral shop industry had peaks around holidays, certainly, but she wasn't sure if there was such a thing as a typical week.

She asked her aunt, "Did Grandma Maude see any pattern to business when she was alive? She did this so many years that she must have figured out something."

Aunt Doris replied, "Yes and no. For a while, she tried being closed on Mondays because business seemed slower on those days, but she discovered that when people die over the weekend, the family wants to order flowers on Mondays. They don't want to wait till Tuesday, even if the funeral isn't till later in the week. So she went back to being open on Mondays and didn't try that experiment again."

"That makes sense. And I suppose being open a half day on Monday didn't work either. Did she try that?"

"No, but I bet you could try working a half day on Saturdays and opening a little later on Monday."

Christie pursed her lips and furrowed her brow. "I like that idea. We could do a trial of being open from ten to two on Saturdays and eleven to five on Mondays, or something like that."

Aunt Doris nodded, humming as she worked on several tabletop arrangements for a dinner party at the private golf club up the road. "That's workable. You know I don't want to work on Saturdays anymore, but maybe Heather would like to help you like you used to help Maude in your high school days."

Christie eyes sparkled. "I was thinking the same thing about Heather. It would give her some spending money, and she'd gain some retail experience at the same time."

"And if she's as good as I think she'll be, you can leave her in charge for a short time while you go to the bank or out to lunch."

"Let's give it a try, Aunt Doris. I'll update the website and see about a sign for the front door with the new hours. I'm sure Anita will help me create something nice."

Aunt Doris smiled, happy that Christie was already comfortable with making adjustments on her own.

~

SEVERAL CUSTOMERS WERE BROWSING in the store when it was near closing time. Christie busied herself with getting the shop ready for the morning while waiting to see if any of them were going to purchase anything.

Her high school English teacher, now retired, walked toward the register with several small items in her hand.

"Hello, Mrs. Fremmerlid," said Christie. "Can I ring these up for you?"

"Yes, please. Christie, you have some great gift items here. But you know, I'm surprised that you came back to White Castle. You were always headed for a big city."

Christie blushed, recalling how emphatic she had been in high school about never coming back to her hometown. "Life has its surprises, and deciding to take over Grandma O'Mara's shop was one of them. Anyway, it's so nice to see you here. You're looking great. Are you enjoying retirement?"

"It took a year or so to get used to sleeping later in the morning and not having to make lesson plans or correct papers." Her ample chest heaved. "But I finally have the time to do what I've wanted to do for years."

"And what is that? By the way, your total today is forty-six dollars and thirty-five cents. I can gift wrap these for you if you like."

"Yes, that would be nice. They're for my granddaughter, who's turning eighteen next week." She handed her credit card to Christie. "Anyway, I've always wanted to write a novel, so I took a couple of classes at the community college."

"Writing a book! Wow! What genre did you choose?" Christie's hands flew as she wrapped the three gifts using beautiful wrapping paper and coordinating ribbon.

"Science fiction, if you can believe that. I tried writing a romance novel and realized right away that it wasn't for me, even if it's a huge industry. Our instructor encouraged us to write what we enjoyed reading. I had to admit that I was a big fan of Ray Bradbury books and *The Twilight Zone* on television, so I started a book about being stranded on an island and waking up in the future in outer space."

"That sounds interesting. Are you finished with it?"

"More or less. Now I'm learning about self-publishing. One of my younger author friends is helping me with getting the right cover and all that. It's certainly a novel experience, pun intended." Mrs. Fremmerlid chuckled. "You do beautiful gift-wrapping, young lady."

"Thank you. My mom taught me." Christie put the packages in a small bag and handed it to her former teacher. "I would never have pegged you as a fan of science fiction. Once you get that book published, I'd be thrilled to sell it in my store."

Mrs. Fremmerlid reddened. "That's sweet of you. I'll take you up on that. Thank you for wrapping these. I'm sure Peyton will love these things. And I wish you great success with your store. You were always a go-getter in high school."

Christie followed Mrs. Fremmerlid to the door. After ascertaining that the other browsers had left, she locked it and flipped the "Open" sign to "Closed." She was turning around to take care of the main light switch when she caught motion out of the corner of her eye and saw Jason jump out of a car that was parked directly in front of her shop. She unlocked the door and held it open as he walked briskly toward the shop.

"Christie, can I talk to you for a minute?" he asked. His breath fogged up in the frosty air.

"Sure, Jason. Come on in, and let me lock the door behind you."

"I couldn't wait to tell you that I found some old court cases in Mr. Thompson's file cabinet. One of them is about that Arnold Youngman you asked about."

CHAPTER

TWENTY-ONE

"You're kidding," said Christie as she locked the door, careful to be sure that it was fully latched. "Follow me while I take care of the lights."

Jason followed Christie to her work counter, where she flipped the main light switch off. The lighting in the back half of the store was operated with a separate switch and remained on even when the store was closed.

"Tell me what you learned," said Christie. "I'm dying of curiosity."

"It turns out that your victim, Arnold Youngman, wasn't from White Castle or even this county. He was from a small town further north, just west of Centralia. I'd never heard of Adna and had to look it up on the map. He had cousins here, so he spent some time here in the summer. I suppose that's how your aunt knew about him."

Christie shook her curls. "Adna? Is it really a town?"

"Yes, but tiny. Probably came to be in the heyday of the timber industry and stayed small because of its lack of other industry."

"Okay. That would explain why there wasn't an obituary in our local paper. So, what else did you learn? Why was Arnold Youngman in those old files?"

"Well, back in 1982, when this all happened, Mr. Thompson was the only attorney in town. He was young and fairly new but had already gotten a good reputation from another case he managed. So he ended up being the defense attorney for the trial, which was held at the county courthouse down the freeway. His notes say he believed that his client, the man who was convicted of killing Arnold Youngman, was innocent. There were two other suspects who the defendant swore were the ones who actually swung the cue stick that killed Mr. Youngman. They were never located."

"You're killing me, Jason. Did you find the names of the suspects?"

"That's what's so interesting. One of them was Jerry Ferguson, the man who died after getting your flowers the other day."

"No way." Christie felt her heart racing.

"Yes. And the other one was someone named Brian Stone. He and Jerry Ferguson never faced charges. They disappeared and got off scot-free. Only Bronco Carver paid the price, and Mr. Thompson felt bad about how it ended."

"Jerry Ferguson may have gotten off then, but he's sure dead now. But is his death connected to that old case? And if it is, why did he come back here?"

"Hey. It's been forty years. He may have assumed that he was safe with statutes of limitations expiring, or maybe he just got tired of hiding."

"Is there a time limit on murder? As in statute of limitations?"

"Not in the state of Washington. He could have been

charged and prosecuted if someone recognized him and reported him to the police or sheriff."

"Wow. So the other suspect, this Brian guy, is still at risk of being charged?"

"Yes, if he's ever found."

Christie frowned. "But someone else has been tried and convicted. Can they really do a do-over like that?"

"Actually, yes. If there's enough evidence to try someone else, they could do so, and if found guilty, the first conviction would be set aside."

"Just like on television."

Jason nodded, a wry smile on his face. "Sort of."

"Hmm. It makes me wonder...never mind." Christie decided to keep the second strange order of flowers to herself. "Hmm. Did you come up with anything that would explain the note I found in the desk? The desk got stolen, by the way, when someone broke into my shop during the night."

"A burglary! I'm so sorry. Are you okay? Was there anything else stolen? Was the note you told me about still in the desk?"

"I'm okay, thanks. The burglary happened during the wee hours of the night, so I was home. Only the desk was taken as far as I could tell, but I'd already removed the note, if that's what they were looking for."

"An old desk is a strange item to steal in a break-in. You're sure nothing else was taken?"

"Not that I could see, although they dumped my files like they were looking for something else. Maybe the note, if that's what they were trying to find in the first place."

"Where is it now? I'm assuming you still have it."

"Yes. I've had it at home, but I'd like to give it to you to keep at your office, in case they come back to look again. Would that be okay?"

"Sure. I have an office safe where I can store it for you."

"Thanks, Jason." Christie leaned over and placed a small kiss on his cheek. She reached into her tote and found the envelope, then pulled out the note. "I just thought of something. The person who wrote this signed it with the initial 'B.' Do you suppose that could be this Brian guy?" She handed the note to Jason, who read it for himself.

"That's an interesting thought. It's certainly possible, I suppose. But it could also be Bronco Carver. What else do you know about the situation?"

"You mean as to this note?"

"Yes."

"Well, I think the 'Missy' might have been a young woman named Teresa Stewart. A neighbor of my parents told me that all the guys had the hots for her, and her nickname was 'Missy.'"

"If Missy is really Teresa and B is Brian or Bronco, that could explain a bit anyway." Jason folded the note carefully and put it back into the envelope before placing it into the inside pocket of his overcoat.

"Right. It might tell us who they are, but I'm not sure it explains enough," said Christie. "Why was this note in the desk in the first place? Who put it there? Why did someone break into my shop and steal the desk? Why does it matter forty years later?"

Jason nodded. "I'll share what I've learned with Chief Conway tomorrow. If Bronco Carver was truly innocent, there may still be a murderer out there."

"If it was Jerry Ferguson, he's already dead. Could it be the other suspect, the man named Brian?" Jason lifted a shoulder.

"If Bronco was innocent, and he's the person who signed the note to Missy, it wouldn't be logical for him to have stolen the desk. I wouldn't expect him to even know what Missy had done with it in the first place."

"Unless Missy told him."

"That could have happened, but when and why?" Christie leaned on her elbows next to her iPad register. "Why did Missy conceal the note in the desk in the first place? Did *she* have something to hide? Do you suppose her parents didn't know she was seeing Bronco and wanted to keep it a secret?"

"You said you think you know who Missy was," said Jason. "Have you tried to track her down?"

"Not yet. I was focused on finding out more about the murder itself. But that's a good idea. I'll talk to Anita about it. That could be our next tactic."

"You know, I worry about you playing detective if there's a chance you could rattle someone's cage enough to come after you. This is a small town, and you never know who might be keeping an eye on you and your killer flowers."

Christie playfully slugged Jason in the arm. "Better watch out, or I'll send some of those to *you*."

"Kidding, of course," said Jason as he pulled away. "Anyway, I'll put this note in the safe for you. I need to get going to a meeting."

Christie let Jason out the front door and reset the lock. She verified that her cameras were set to record, collected her kitty and tote, and left via the back door after arming her alarm. Finally, she carefully secured the new lock that had been installed by her father after he had finished repairing the broken glass in the door, this time with wire embedded in the pane.

CHAPTER

TWENTY-TWO

Christie fed Stormy before picking up the phone to call Anita. Perhaps because she'd been a stray, the kitty was quite insistent about her dinner being ready practically the minute Christie stepped foot in the house. She communicated her needs by purring loudly and rubbing her warm body against Christie's legs until her kibble bowl was next to the water bowl on the mat.

"You're a good kitty," said Christie as she warmed up her own dinner, yummy leftover chicken marsala courtesy of her mom. "I wish you could tell me why you hiss at some of my customers, although I tend to agree with you so far." Christie reached down to scratch behind Stormy's ears. "I'm glad you approve of Jason. He seems like a warm, friendly guy now that he's a grown-up. Funny how people can be so different from what we thought in high school." She looked off into space and smiled.

Cat fed and a glass of wine poured for herself, Christie curled up with her feet under her on the newly recovered armchair that had been her grandma's and dialed her friend.

"Hey, Anita. How's life in your blackboard jungle? Or maybe I should call it a whiteboard jungle with all the electronic boards these days."

"Funny *not*," Anita said, an edge to her voice. "I've had one lousy day. One of my male students has been making suggestive comments in class, and I asked him to stop, or I'd send him to the principal's office."

"That tactic worked when *we* were students," said Christie. "What happened?"

Anita sighed. "Well, today I found out he's been posting a bunch of stuff about me on Facebook, and it's not very nice. Among other things, he posted a suggestive picture with my head superimposed on it. I went to the principal, and of course, he called the parents to come in after school. Turns out this smart aleck has a wimpy mother who is clueless about what to do and an obnoxious dad who couldn't care less. We were there for a long forty-five minutes."

"How did it turn out?"

"The kid is suspended for a week and has to take down the postings. Unfortunately, there isn't another class that he can transfer into, so he'll be back in my classroom next week." She groaned, and Christie pictured an eye roll. "Maybe his parents will send him to a virtual academy or move out of town."

"Not very likely, but you can always hope."

"Yeah, I know. I've got my fingers crossed. So why'd you call? I'm sure it wasn't to hear about my bad day."

"Well, do you remember my telling you that my neighbor Jack said that there was a girl in town back in the early eighties who was called Missy? Her real name was Teresa Stewart, and she may have been the girlfriend of Arnold Youngman, the man who died after the bar fight. From what I've learned so far, she disappeared about the time of the trial, as did the two other suspects."

"So?"

"What if she wasn't *Arnold's* girlfriend but was actually seeing the guy who was tried and convicted? His name was Bronco Carver. Bronco starts with the letter 'B,' and it makes more sense that he would be proclaiming his innocence to her if he's worried he's going to end up in jail."

"Okay. But is Bronco even someone's real name? I'm following your logic, such as it is, but why is that important now?"

"Last night, someone broke the window in the back door at the store and stole that writing desk. Nothing else was taken, although they dumped my file drawers and a couple of flower tubs. It made me wonder if they were trying to disguise what else they were looking for."

"Oh, I'm so sorry to hear that. Were you able to pull up images from the cameras and catch the thief in the act?"

"Unfortunately, I didn't set them properly, so they didn't record anything."

"What do you mean? I showed you how to—"

"I know, I know, and I'm sorry, but obviously, I'm not a very good listener." She didn't want to tell her friend that the instructions Anita left were a bit too cryptic for someone unfamiliar with such things. "Anyway, Police Chief Conway came by today and reviewed how to do it correctly from now on. But it made me wonder about Missy or Bronco, and whether he's the one who wrote the note if one of them had come back to town and is trying to recover it for some reason."

"But why risk doing something illegal and ending up in jail? Wouldn't it make more sense to ask directly?"

"Hmm. You'd think so, but maybe it's not Missy or Bronco but one of the other suspects who wants to find the note, because it could be evidence that clears Bronco's name."

"But you said the note didn't name anyone."

"True, but if Bronco was innocent — and the attorney of record apparently thought so, according to Jason — there's still an unsolved murder, and there's no statute of limitations on murder in the state of Washington. At least, I think that's what Jason was saying."

"How does Jason know what the attorney thought?"

"He came by the store at closing time today and told me that he'd found the case file for Bronco Carver. When Jason bought Mr. Thompson's law practice, he agreed to store all the old files, which dated back about fifty years. He searched through them and found out that Mr. Thompson had been the defense attorney for Mr. Carver. In his notes, Mr. Thompson wrote that he believed his client to be innocent and felt bad that he hadn't been able to clear him. He named the other two suspects as well. And one of them was Jerry Ferguson, the man who died after he got that bouquet from my shop."

"But I thought I heard he had a heart attack."

"What if something triggered that heart attack? Like old bad news?"

"What bad news?"

"I'm not sure, but what if someone had told him they knew Bronco Carver had been innocent, and they had evidence that would put him, Jerry Ferguson, in jail? And I just had a thought — what if Bronco Carver himself showed up at his door, looking for revenge? He should have been released from jail about fifteen years ago or earlier if he got time off for good behavior."

"Yeah, but what does that have to do with Teresa Stewart?"

Christie sighed. Anita was right — what did any of this have to do with anything else? But something niggled at Christie's brain, like something needed to be cleared up before she could let it go. "Maybe nothing, but perhaps she *does* know something, and that's why she disappeared before the trial. I want to find her. I want to ask her about the note and who sent it to her."

"Okay, girlfriend. How can I help you?"

"Here's what I'm thinking. If she was a local girl and was in her early twenties in 1982 when this all happened, she would have been a student at White Castle High School in the seventies, like 1974 to 1978 or thereabouts. I'm hoping you can have someone check student records and maybe find an address and her parents' names. And if she had siblings who might still be around."

"Christie, that's not as easy as you make it sound. Forty years ago, those records were almost certainly handwritten and are probably in cardboard boxes somewhere, if they haven't been destroyed."

"Doesn't the school keep those records forever? Could they be on microfiche, like the newspapers at the library?"

"Maybe. I'll ask at the office. But don't get your hopes up. I might be denied access."

"Hadn't thought of that. Well, all you can do is give it a shot. And I'll ask Aunt Doris if she remembers anything. Sometimes her memory is clear, but other times I wonder if she's developing short-term memory loss, in addition to being a little goofy in the first place."

"Your aunt must be pushing eighty by now, isn't she? You know it's not uncommon to have memory issues in that age group."

"I know. And sometimes, I wonder if she's holding back information on purpose. Like she's afraid of something happening to me."

TWENTY-THREE

Christie settled in at her kitchen table and fired up her Mac, grateful her father had helped her install internet service at her home. She was intent on learning something about the mysterious Teresa Stewart, hoping there was a snippet of information that would help locate her whereabouts.

She started with a yearbook search but soon hit a dead end. It seemed no one had uploaded the White Castle High School yearbooks from the years when Teresa had most likely, if at all, attended school there. Then she tried a property title search but didn't have any better luck. A random Google search turned up at least forty women named Teresa Stewart with various spellings of both Teresa and Stewart, but none with obvious local connections.

With a second glass of cabernet sauvignon poured, Christie perused the obituaries for the tri-county area. Maybe Teresa had died young. It happened sometimes. When Christie was a freshman in high school, a senior girl died in a freak sled-meets-car accident over the winter break. Christie recalled how the students had been called to the school auditorium for a memorial service a day or two after school resumed in January. But she didn't find an obituary for Teresa. Christie hoped Anita would have better luck with the school office. If she could identify even one bit of useful information, she might be able to find the missing "Missy."

TUESDAY MORNING DAWNED dry and sunny but with a crispness in the air. The old adage, *the frost is on the pumpkin,* came to mind when she noted the temperature on the thermometer hanging on the outside of her garage was thirty-three degrees. She looked at it every morning from her kitchen window and dressed accordingly. This day would call for a scarf, hat and gloves if she were going to be outside any length of time.

She arrived at her store twenty minutes prior to opening to find her aunt bustling around, a handful of orders in her hand, while checking the cooler for flower stock.

"It looks like you managed to disarm the alarm successfully, Auntie," she said as she hung up her things.

"I was a little nervous but I followed your instructions exactly and held my breath. I didn't want to have an unnecessary police visit triggered by me."

Christie giggled. "Fortunately, I get a couple of freebies for unintentional alarms, so don't worry."

"Good to know. Say, did you order more baby's breath and eucalyptus to replace what we lost from the break-in?"

"Yes, I did. And I also added more of that *Alstroemeria* in the pretty coral shade you liked. They should be delivered today from the Portland distributor."

"Perfect. I'll work on the orders that don't need those fillers until the delivery arrives later."

Christie made cups of Earl Gray tea for herself and her aunt.

"Here's a cup of your favorite tea, Auntie."

"Why, thank you, Honey. That's sweet of you." Aunt Doris took a swallow of the warm brew and picked up a pair of scissors to cut off the ends of the flower stems in her hand.

Christie stood next to the work table and swallowed hard before asking the question she'd prepared. "When I asked you about Teresa Stewart a few days ago, I sensed that you knew more than you were willing to tell me."

Doris turned and narrowed her eyes, then smiled and continued snipping away. "What makes you think that? It was a long time ago, and my memory isn't as sharp as it used to be."

"I think you're still pretty sharp. What do you know that you're not telling me? Please. It's important. And I have to unlock the front door in a few minutes."

Doris's chest heaved, and she laid her scissors on the work table. She looked up to the ceiling before saying, "Keep in mind that what I'm about to tell you was a rumor at the time. It was never confirmed to my knowledge, but back then, this kind of thing was still hush-hush in a little town like this."

"Go on. I'm listening."

"Okay. The word around town was that Teresa got herself pregnant. Shoulda known better with birth control pills and all that, of course. Anyway, some folks thought that Arnold Youngman, the man who died after that bar fight, was the father, but others swore that it was Bronco Carver. And that the fight was about the baby."

"That could make sense! But what happened to her after that?"

"That's another part I don't know. I've wondered all these years myself. Maybe she wasn't sure who the father was, or whoever it was didn't want to marry her. Of course, one was dead and the other imprisoned, so marriage wasn't in the cards anyway. So, maybe she had an abortion. Maybe she had the child and gave it up for adoption. Maybe she was never pregnant. But we never saw her around here again."

Christie glanced at the front door when she noticed a shadow out of the corner of her eye. She hugged her aunt, saying, "Thank you for sharing, Aunt Doris. I'm going to keep looking for her. There's our first customer. I'll get the door."

ANITA CALLED during her lunch break. "I got lucky when I asked about school records from the seventies. The school administration secretary told me that about twenty years ago, the superintendent decided to digitalize all that old student information. And they paid some college kids to come in and do the scanning and data entry work during the summer."

"And?"

"Turns out that Teresa Stewart wasn't a student at White Castle High according to the online records, but she *was* a student teacher for one quarter in 1982. She helped in Mrs. Fremmerlid's English classes."

"If she wasn't a student, how did you find that out?"

"The teachers for those years were also listed, as well as teachers' aides. She was filed under that category. All I had to do was search for her name, and it popped up."

"That's really interesting," said Christie. "Mrs. Fremmerlid was in my shop a day or two ago buying some gifts. I had no idea she might have been able to help me with this."

"She's retired now, isn't she?"

"Oh, yes. I think she retired soon after we graduated. Our class might have worn her out." Christie giggled.

"Or maybe it was because her son graduated a year or two later, and it was good timing for her."

"That, too," acknowledged Christie. "Did you learn anything else about Teresa? Like where she was from or where she attended college?"

"Yes, and no. She was apparently from somewhere around Centralia, but her college information wasn't listed."

"Centralia isn't that big a town. I'll see if I can track her family down. Thanks, Anita. I'll buy you a glass of wine next time we get together."

"I'd like that. Gotta go. Time to go back to my students and the whiteboard jungle."

Christie pocketed her phone and walked back to help her aunt with one of the orders.

"That was Anita. She said Teresa Stewart was from Centralia and was a student teacher back in the early eighties. I'm going to ask Mrs. Fremmerlid if she remembers anything about her."

"Hmm," said her aunt. "Didn't you tell me that one of those boys in the bar fight was from Adna? That dinky town isn't very far from there. Maybe that's how they knew each other."

TWENTY-FOUR

Christie felt restless that evening once she got home from work. Loose ends flitted through her brain, one of which was tracking down Lynette Nichols. Christie wondered why she hadn't returned to purchase the writing desk after the initial attempt. And who broke into the store to steal it? The only person who had expressed any interest in it had been Lynette. She didn't appear to be the type of person to be a thief, but then again, she hadn't seemed the type to try to manipulate a small-town retailer on a price either. Stormy slept in a kitty bed next to the fireplace with its crackling warmth, oblivious to Christie's silent mulling.

She turned her television to *Jeopardy* and unsuccessfully tried to keep her attention on the program. One of the topics was English literature of the nineteenth century, which prompted Christie to call her former teacher, Mrs. Fremmerlid, before it got too late to call.

"Mrs. Fremmerlid? This is Christie O'Mara from the flower shop. Do you have a minute?"

"What a surprise to hear from you! What's on your mind, Christie?"

"I'm calling to ask if you remember a student teacher named Teresa Stewart. She would have been in your classroom in the early eighties, maybe 1982."

The phone was silent for a moment before Mrs. Fremmerlid replied, "I had to stop and think. That was a long time ago. As I recall, her real name was Teresa, but we all called her 'Missy.' She just didn't look like a Teresa, if you know what I mean, and that's what she said her family called her. Is that the right one?"

"Yes," said Christie, sitting up straighter. "Do you know what happened to her after she left White Castle?"

"Well, let's see now. She was finishing up her bachelor's degree in education at Western Washington University, as I recall. And was planning to apply for a teaching job anywhere she could get one. No, that's not right. She told me she had decided to take some time off before starting her career. I tried to convince her to apply for jobs for the fall semester, but she was quite adamant that she was not going to apply for a job here, even though I'm sure there were openings."

"Did she say why?"

"I'm not sure I asked, but she mentioned that she had family in Spokane and might apply for a job in that area once she had settled in."

"Did you follow through to find out what happened to her?"

"I never checked," she replied, sighing. "I always thought she would be a great teacher, though, so I hope she landed somewhere."

"Thank you so much, Mrs. Fremmerlid. That gives me a place to start."

"You didn't tell me why you're asking about her."

"I hope she can tell me more about a letter I found at the shop."

"A letter?"

"Well, more like a note. I'll tell you the rest of the story if I find her."

"All right. Well, I'm going to sit down and write a few more words in my novel before I go to bed. I watched a webinar today about world-building, and it made me think of something I could do differently. Anyway, I'm glad you called. It was nice to chat with you."

Christie curled her legs under her and pulled a fleece throw over her shoulders. She had been writing notes related to the writing desk mystery in a spiral notebook that she kept on the end table next to her. She picked it up and jotted down the information she'd obtained from Anita earlier, as well as what she'd just learned from Mrs. Fremmerlid. If Aunt Doris had been correct about a pregnancy, that could be why Missy was delaying starting a teaching job. She thumbed through the pages, hoping the missing link to the puzzle would magically materialize. She also had a small stack of other notes from work and the library, and the picture from her yearbook. She studied the picture of Lynette and tried to imagine what she would look like now if she were to apply the aging technology like the experts do for missing children. She suddenly realized that the name was spelled differently than the name on Lynette's credit card.

The yearbook photo of Lynette Somers spelled her first name Linette, not Lynette. It couldn't be the same woman who'd admired the desk. Christie's shoulders sagged. So, who was Lynette Nichols? And was she connected to the note? Or not?

Christie started a list of names on another piece of paper. Brian Stone, Jerry Ferguson and Bronco Carver were connected to the bar fight. Jerry was dead, maybe because of the killer flowers. She still had to find Brian and Bronco. Teresa aka Missy Stewart and Brian — or maybe Bronco — were Missy and B, she thought. Lynette Nichols might somehow be related to the desk and to the note. Was it really Lynette's grandmother's desk? Or was it one that just resembled it, like the woman had said? And who stole the desk? She felt confident that it was someone who hoped to find that note. Why else lug something like that desk out in a burglary? But was the thief the note's author? Or the recipient? Or someone else who knew about it and was worried about what it said?

Christie sighed and took another swallow of her wine.

TWENTY-FIVE

Wednesday's morning temperature had dropped down to thirty, which was typical in November when there were no clouds overnight to seal in the earth's warmth. Christie hurried through her morning routine, partly because she wanted to get to the store early and partly because moving faster helped her to warm up. Stormy didn't seem to want to leave her cozy blanket in front of the kitchen heater vent.

Christie had slept restlessly, her mind going back to Brian and Bronco. Where were they now? She hoped Jason, with his legal connections, could discover where Bronco went after he was released from prison. She figured he had likely served less than the full term of twenty-five years if he'd earned good behavior credit. And if he was truly innocent, that might well be the case. Finding Brian Stone would be harder. She didn't know if he had been a local boy, or someone working in town who lived elsewhere, or even someone just passing through who decided to have a beer at the bar.

"Stormy, I'm sorry to disturb you, but I'm not going to let you stay here by yourself. You might get bored and find something to claw on, and then I'll be mad at you." Christie put a jeweled pink leather harness around the kitty's torso and bribed Stormy into the cat carrier. "That's a good kitty. We need to go to work, and then I'll call Jason. I have an idea I hope he'll help me with."

Christie was at the shop before her aunt, which was unusual and not likely to be repeated very often. Aunt Doris was definitely an early bird and prided herself on being at the shop and already working away when her boss walked in. She'd been that way with her own sister-in-law Maude as well, as Christie recalled from her summer work.

Stormy hopped up to her favorite shelf above the register and began preening herself as though she knew her "subjects" would be arriving soon. Christie took care of the morning opening routine, then placed a phone call to Jason's office while waiting for Doris to appear.

"Christie! I didn't expect to hear from you so soon, but I'm glad you called."

"Good morning, Jason. Do you have a minute?"

"For you, absolutely."

"Okay. Remember when we talked about the note in the desk?"

"Of course. It's sitting in my office safe as we speak."

"Well, last night I was thinking about who would try to break into my shop and take the desk. If that lady Lynette had taken it on my opening day when she wanted to buy it, it wouldn't have even been in my shop. I don't know if I told you that her credit card failed like three times, and she didn't have enough cash, so she was planning to come back a couple of days later, the next Monday, to pay for it."

"And apparently, she didn't follow through."

"Correct. Just a second. Aunt Doris just came in." Christie covered the phone with her hand while calling out to her aunt. "Hi, Auntie. I'm on the phone for a minute. Can you get the front door?"

Aunt Doris saluted with her free hand, set down her purse and hung her coat.

"Thank you, Auntie." To Jason, she said, "She never came back, not even the next day. If she knew about the note, I would think she would have been here early Monday to pay for the desk and take it home. Although, I do wonder how she thought she would get it home in that Porsche."

"I would guess she didn't expect to find it in your shop in the first place," said Jason.

"I agree. But she didn't come back. I find it hard to believe she would break in to steal it. As far as she knew, I would still be holding it for her."

"You don't think she's the 'Missy' of the note, do you?"

"At first I did, but not anymore. She's much too young, but it crossed my mind that she could be *related* to Missy some-how. Like, her daughter? She would be about the right age for that but too old to be Missy's granddaughter. Anyway, I made a list last night of the other people who conceivably could know about the desk as well as the note. Missy, for one, if she's still alive. Bronco, if he's the 'B' who wrote the note and someone told him where it was. It could even be the guy iden-tified as Brian in the court files if he was the signer of the note. Because we don't know. It could have been either one of them."

"Would you like me to do some detective work for you? I know someone who is a specialist in finding 'lost' people. He tracks down heirs of people who've died and has helped adopted children find their birth mothers and that sort of thing. He owes me a favor, and this might be just the way he could pay me back and help you."

"Oh, Jason! That would be amazing if he can find Teresa Stewart or Brian Stone or Bronco Carver, or all three."

"Consider it done, my friend. I'll call him today and see what other information he might need to get started."

CHAPTER

TWENTY-SIX

For a Wednesday morning in November, the shop was busier than usual. There were smiling browsers, plus the delivery of an armload of orders for a funeral to be held on Saturday. Christie used a free moment to check the flower cooler for calla lilies and chrysanthemums. Chrysanthemums were versatile and added a touch of soft color when other flowers were no longer in season or were unavailable. Florists often use white calla lilies for funerals because the color has come to represent angels or purity.

Christie smiled to herself as she imagined what a pastor might say at the funeral service about someone who had been known to be something of a scamp or worse. Would he cross his fingers under his robe or behind his back?

The front door chimed, announcing a customer. Christie looked up to see Chief Conway in her doorway again.

"Good afternoon, Chief," Christie said cheerfully. "Are you here to order flowers today?"

Conway took his hat off and leaned with his elbow on the order counter, his face sober. "We found this at the residence

126

of a deceased man today." He handed her a floral card labeled with Christie's flower shop business. He scrolled to a photo on his phone and held it out for her. "Do you recall who ordered these flowers?"

Doris peeked over Christie's shoulder and gasped. "I knew that order was bad news. We should have said 'No' when he called."

Christie said, "No, I don't know who the gentleman was, but he had a raspy voice like the first man who ordered flowers for someone who ended up dead. I told you about that when you came in last weekend, and I showed you the video of the man who picked up the order."

"Hmm. So a man with a raspy voice orders these flowers, and a second victim dies. It's unlikely that two different men are ordering the flowers, so it seems there must be some connection to the recipients." Conway looked at Christie. "Any ideas as to what that would be?"

Christie shrugged. "I wish I knew, but I'm clueless."

"What about these mysterious messages? How does your raspy-voiced man know what they mean?"

"Well, there is a list of flower meanings on my website, but it only lists a few of the most common ones. But anyone could look up that kind of information online if they want to do so."

"I suppose that could have happened."

"Do you have any idea what the connection could be between the recipients? I don't know the name of the second gentleman, but I'm sure you'll be asking his family if they know of any possibility."

"Of course." Conway pocketed his notes and said, "That's all I have for now. I'll let you know if I have any more questions."

Christie sighed. "This isn't going to be good for business. I can see the headline now: 'Killer Flowers Strike Again.'"

Stormy jumped down from her perch and positioned herself between Christie and the police chief. She purred and rubbed her head against Conway's arm that was resting on the counter. Conway stroked the smooth black fur with his other hand.

"That reminds me of something," said Christie. "When this man, now deceased as you say, came in to pick up those flowers, Stormy hissed at him. She had hissed at the first Mr. Jones also."

Conway chuckled. "Do you think your cat has some kind of power to pick out bad guys or something?"

"No, but she does seem to make a point of letting me know when she doesn't like someone. I don't know what she senses or how she decides."

"Well, I'm glad she seems to like me." Conway smiled as Stormy continued purring and pushing her head into his hand.

"Oh, since you're here, I have another question. Do you have any leads on my stolen desk?"

"Sorry. Nothing. That's the kind of item that might show up on eBay, craigslist or Facebook Marketplace if someone's trying to make a few dollars off it. Although, to be honest, from what you described, it isn't like a Chippendale or something really valuable. So stealing something that big in order to resell it doesn't seem likely." He ended with a shrug.

She had to laugh at his rather puzzled shrug. It seemed even the authorities were simply baffled at times. "Yes, one more riddle."

CHAPTER
TWENTY-SEVEN

Jason popped into the shop just before one o'clock with a manila envelope in his hand. Christie looked up from her desk, where she was filling out an order form online. She smiled and stood behind the counter.

"You're grinning, Jason. I bet you found something and couldn't wait to tell me."

Jason opened the envelope and slid the contents onto the counter's surface. Stormy jumped down from her shelf and forced her head under his arm. "She seems to like me," he said, grinning as he scratched behind the kitty's ear.

Christie had already picked up the first page and started reading. "This is interesting. So Mrs. Fremmerlid was right. Teresa Stewart was indeed pregnant." She looked up at Jason. "But she gave the baby up for adoption?"

"That's what it looks like."

Didn't you mention something about Spokane after you talked with Mrs. Fremmerlid? That she had family there?"

"Yes, so it would make sense that she would stay there,

have the baby, and no one here would be the wiser. Then she could start teaching."

Jason nodded. "That's how I interpret that bit of information."

"Did your private investigator find out anything about the baby?"

"Only that it was a girl, and she would be about forty now."

"What if the lady who wanted the desk was that daughter?" Christie leaned on her elbow against the counter, chin in her hand. She sighed. "I hope there's more to that story."

"There is. Teresa was the youngest of the family, with three brothers. I can imagine they were interested in protecting her honor and were instrumental in her disappearing with hardly a trace."

"Okay, so what else do you have for me?"

"Here's what the PI found out about Bronco Carver. He was released early from the state penitentiary after twenty years due to good behavior, went to trade school, and has been working in the Easton area since then as an electrician."

"Hmm. Just a thought, but could an electrician kill people with some kind of electrical shock?"

"I think you watched too many science fiction movies, Christie." Jason shook his head at her suggestion.

"Well, it's certainly interesting that he ended up practically in his original backyard," said Christie. "Did he ever get married?"

"He had a brief marriage about five years out of prison, but it didn't work out. That's as much as my associate has found out."

"Well, thank you for this information. It doesn't fill in the answers to all my questions, but I appreciate getting this far. I wonder if he's still in Easton." Christie replaced the pages in the envelope and started to give it back to Jason.

"You can keep it. My PI is still asking questions. Right now, I need to get back to work. I have a client to see at one thirty."

"I owe you," Christie said as Jason headed to the door.

"Dinner Friday night," he called over his shoulder. "You're cooking." He paused a moment, then turned to look at her, waiting for a response.

"You're on." She smiled.

Christie hummed a happy tune while she finished the order she'd started earlier. She was pleased that the gift items were selling so well. She'd lucked into finding a line of goods that were of good quality, cute, and reasonably priced — just the right fit for her small town with mostly average incomes. She had planned to have an eclectic but affordable mix of vases and figurines and other table toppers such that her customers could find something without having to travel to the larger city just up the freeway. So far, it seemed to be working.

"What's that song you're humming?" asked Aunt Doris. "And isn't that three times that the Princeton kid has stopped by the store?" She winked at her niece.

Christie felt her skin redden. "I'm not counting, Auntie. And it's business."

"Sure, it is. Well, I'm glad. It gives you something to do besides count your money."

"Hey, Auntie. Do you have any orders for Heather to deliver today? She's available."

"I was just about to tell you that two of these orders need to go out this afternoon. They're both just outside the city limits, but one goes north and the other goes south, opposite directions." Doris handed her the address labels.

Christie read them and said, "I'll ask Heather to take the one to Morrow Road. She lives that direction anyway, and I'll go to Laurel Place. It's not far out of my way home."

"Sounds perfect."

The rest of the afternoon raced by as the two women worked side by side creating beautiful arrangements for a couple of birthdays, an anniversary, and a baby shower, as well as a tabletop display for the bereaved family. They would make up the funeral flower arrangements on Friday.

Christie's cell phone buzzed in her pocket. She wiped her wet hands before answering. "Hi, Anita. What's up?"

"I'm free this evening if you are. Do you want to meet somewhere for dinner?"

"Sounds like a great idea! You must have known I'm out of my mom's leftovers. Where do you think we should go?"

"I've heard that the Lemon Drop has good food and decent wine prices, if you don't mind driving ten miles up the road to Carrolton. I've been wanting to try it."

"Is seven good?"

"See you then. I'll pick you up at your house."

TWENTY-EIGHT

"This isn't what I expected with a name like Lemon Drop," said Christie, standing just inside the door of the former brewery, which had been converted into a more sophisticated cafe. "I was worried it would be really frou-frou."

"My friend Angela told me that the owner has plans to do more tweaking but decided to wait to do more expensive remodeling until next summer," Anita explained. "She wanted to be sure her business was stable before spending that kind of money. The food is great, I hear."

A smiling waitress showed them to a round table in the corner and told them about the evening's specials. The menu tended toward light, vegetable-based items like a Thai lettuce wrap and a selection of fancy cocktails with clever names, such as Nectar of the Goddess.

"I love the food options," said Christie. "And though I would normally drink wine, I'm going to try their Lemon Drop with this noodle dish with chicken."

"The gnocchi sounds good to me," said Anita. "I had some

in Italy a few years ago and like to try it when I see it on a menu. One of these days I'm going to make it, but I haven't been brave enough yet. Do you think a Pom-Pom Drop would go with it?"

Christie giggled. "That sounds a bit like a cheerleader's drink, doesn't it?

"Hey, you were a cheerleader in high school. You should know! On second thought, I'll try the lettuce wrap. It won't be as many calories, I hope."

Once the waitress took their drink and food orders, Christie asked, "Did you have something on your mind when you called?"

Anita grinned and nodded her head. "The high school secretary did some research on her own after I asked about Teresa Stewart. She found her application for that student teaching position and made a copy for me."

"Ooh," Christie squealed. "Does it have her parents' names and an address?"

Anita produced a legal-sized envelope from her tote and handed it to Christie. "Yes. This is for you. I knew you would want to see it. Notice that her parents lived in Centralia."

Christie perused the document, which had been filled out with a typewriter. She chuckled. "It's interesting to see old forms like this. It's almost prehistoric. Anyway, this application would have been from forty years ago, so if she was twenty-two or so at the time, her parents must have been in their late thirties or early forties. Could have been older, especially if she was one of the younger kids. Jason told me this morning that she had three brothers. I'm guessing the parents have to be at least in their late seventies or early eighties now."

"You're also assuming the parents are still alive."

"True. I'll see what I can find on the internet. The Whitepages app on my phone is useful when I'm trying to locate an address or phone number — if they have a landline, that is."

The waitress appeared with two drinks that looked promising. The lemon drop was served in a martini glass with a rim of sugar and a twisted lemon slice. Anita's Pom-Pom was a rich red mimosa with a maraschino cherry floating in a tall flute.

"Cheers, my friend," said Christie.

"And to you," replied Anita, taking a sip. "This is delicious. I would never have thought of using pomegranate in a drink, but combined with the prosecco, it's quite elegant. You know, it's kinda fun to be friends as grown-ups. Less drama than back in high school."

"That's for sure." Christie tasted her drink. "Yum. This is delightful. It's lemony and smooth and not overly sweet."

"Anything new from Jason? You mentioned he was going to do some background checking for you."

The food, with its wonderful aroma, arrived as Christie began telling Anita more of what she'd learned that morning.

"Have you made any phone calls to Easton to try to locate Mr. Carver? There can't be that many businesses that employ electricians, outside of big industries and the power companies." Anita held a bite of her lettuce wrap on her fork. "This is delicious. Really fresh-tasting with the crunch of the lettuce and the smooth texture of the filling. Yum."

Christie speared a piece of chicken and tasted it. "So is this. I wonder what they use for the sauce on the noodles. Anyway, I'll make a few calls tomorrow during my lunch break. From what my father says, men in skilled trades tend to know each other and which company they're working for. I might strike pay dirt quickly."

"And Teresa's parents? They're probably retired, so you could reach them at home if you can find a telephone number."

Christie groaned. "In the days of landlines, it was easier than now trying to track down cell phone numbers. But I'll start with the number on this application. It could work. My own parents still have a landline even though they don't use it most of the time. Dad's argument is that if electricity goes out, and he can't charge a cell phone, he can still use an old-fashioned telephone."

"Makes sense," said Anita. "I hope that's the case with the Stewarts."

STORMY PURRED HAPPILY on Christie's lap in front of the fireplace. Christie crossed her fingers and dialed the Stewarts' phone number, or at least the one they'd had in 1982. One, two, three, then four rings, followed by a click. Christie's shoulders slumped, thinking she was at a dead end. Then she heard a male voice saying, "Hello?"

"Hello, sir, this is Christie O'Mara from White Castle. Is this Mr. Stewart?"

"Yes. Did you say White Castle?"

"Yes, sir. I believe your daughter Teresa did student teaching here in 1982. Is that correct?"

"Just a minute, please. Let me call my wife to the phone."

Christie heard a muffled "Lydia" and then a female voice saying. "This is Teresa's mother. My husband is hard of hearing, but he thought you said you were calling from White Castle."

"Yes, that's correct. I'm trying to locate a Teresa Stewart about a note I found in an old desk at my grandmother's flower shop. If your daughter was also called 'Missy,' she may be the person mentioned in the note."

"I'm not following you. What note? What desk? What flower shop?"

"Was Teresa your daughter, and was she called 'Missy' by your family?"

"Yes, she was our little 'Missy' after we had three rambunctious boys. But I don't understand what note or desk you're talking about."

"Let me explain. About a month ago, I moved back to White Castle to take over my grandmother's flower shop here in town. Anyway, I found a few vintage furniture pieces in her back room and decided to try to sell them. You know, to make a little more money if I didn't sell enough flowers."

"I see."

"One of the items was a lovely cherry writing desk, like in the old days where women used to sit when writing their correspondence and that sort of thing. When I was getting it ready to sell, I found a note taped to the bottom of one of the drawers. It was to someone named 'Missy' and was signed with the letter 'B.' It mentioned a murder and implied that this 'B' guy — at least I think it must have been a guy — was implicated but wasn't guilty and was leaving town without getting a chance to see her."

"And you think this 'Missy' was our daughter? What makes you think that?"

Christie swallowed, her mouth dry. "I did some background checking, and it turns out that a young woman named Teresa Stewart was a student teacher here in 1982. The school records listed you and your husband as her parents. I took a chance and called you."

"I'm quite sure I don't know anything about this desk and a note, and definitely not any murder," said Mrs. Stewart with an icy voice before the phone went dead.

Christie stared at the phone for a moment. Mrs. Stewart

didn't deny that she had a daughter named Teresa, but she certainly didn't fess up to the desk or the note. She stroked the soft black fur of her cat and said, "Stormy, I don't understand, but it looks like it isn't going to be as easy as I thought to connect Teresa-also-known-as-Missy to that desk. I'll have to try a different approach. I think I'll leave the murder out of it next time."

CHAPTER

TWENTY-NINE

The shop's telephone rang multiple times early in the day with additional requests for funeral flowers and several birthday and anniversary bouquets. Christie finally found a few minutes to make some calls to Easton in her quest to find Bronco Carver. She had done some research the evening before and identified several businesses that likely employed electricians, including the Public Utility District. She took a big breath and entered the first number on the list, which was for the county PUD.

After introducing herself and her reason for calling, she was directed to the human resources office.

"Hi, Ms. Norris. I hope you can help me. This is Christie O'Mara from White Castle. I'm looking for a gentleman named Bronco Carver. I was told he might work for your agency as an electrician."

"What would be the reason you're looking for Mr. Carver, if I may ask?" The voice was hoarse, like that of a woman who had smoked too many years.

Christie felt her heart race. She hadn't anticipated having

to explain why she wanted to find him and was hesitant to bring up an old murder. Doing that yesterday hadn't served her well with Mrs. Stewart.

"I want to ask him some questions about a young woman he may have known here in town forty years ago."

"Are you with the police?"

"No, Ma'am. I own a flower shop. I found a note in a desk that I think he might have written to the young woman."

"Well, I can't help you with that. Unfortunately, Mr. Carver retired a couple of years ago."

Christie felt her heart thud. "Oh. Do you have any contact information so I could try him at his home?"

"I'm sure you realize I can't give you his private number, but I could call him myself and see if he wants to contact you."

"That would be great, if you would. Thank you so much." Christie recited her cell phone number and pinched herself. She could hardly wait to tell Anita. She hummed a tune and danced around the shop for a moment before suddenly thinking that Mr. Carver might not want to contact her at all.

"I'll have to wait and see," Christie said to Stormy, who had opened an eye with the sudden commotion. "But I have a feeling he'll contact me. He may have some unfinished business here."

LATE IN THE DAY, Christie's cell buzzed in her pocket. Her heart leapt when she saw an unfamiliar number. Fingers crossed, she answered with, "This is Christie."

"This is Bronco Carver. Thelma Norris from the PUD said you wanted to talk to me."

"Yes, yes! Thank you for calling me. Do you remember a

student teacher in White Castle named Teresa Stewart? You might know her as Missy."

Christie heard a loud exhale and was afraid Mr. Carver was going to hang up on her. Instead, he said, "No, but someone shouted her name that night when I was at that bar. Some idiots were fighting with cue sticks, and I was afraid they were going to kill each other, so I tried to break it up and grabbed the stick from one of them. Unfortunately, someone had called the sheriff, and when he arrived, I was the only one holding a cue stick in my hand. Most everyone had fled the scene, and I was arrested even though I hadn't hit anyone. When that one guy died, I got hit with a murder charge."

"I'm so sorry. One of my friends took over the law practice of your defense attorney. He told me that Mr. Thompson believed you were innocent but couldn't prove it and felt bad about it. Do you remember any of the other eyewitnesses from the night?"

"No. I'm originally from Adna and was working on a construction job there. A couple of buddies from work and I dropped in for a couple of drinks after a long day. I didn't know anybody but them. Having the murder weapon in my hand was the only hard evidence the sheriff had. My word and my buddy's word weren't enough. There were a dozen other men in the bar when the ruckus started, but they pretty much had all scattered by the time the sheriff arrived."

"You mentioned that Missy's name came up. How was that?"

"I didn't hear the conversation directly, but when I asked what the fight was about, two dudes at the bar next to me told me it was about someone named 'Missy.' I didn't know her real name until the trial."

"So you weren't dating her?"

"I didn't know her. So, no."

"Hmm. So you didn't write her a note and send it to her?"

"No, I didn't. I said I didn't know her. Why are you so curious about this anyway? I served my time, and it's all behind me."

Christie thought for a few seconds before telling Bronco about the desk and the note. It crossed her mind that he could conceivably be the murderer or bent on revenge. "I was hoping you were the man who signed the note as 'B,' but it doesn't sound like it's you after all."

"I wish it were. Maybe it would help prove I was innocent after all. But it doesn't really matter anymore."

"It might," said Christie. "If you think about it, there's still a murderer out there who got away with it in 1982. And there's no statute of limitations on murder in this state."

Christie shivered involuntarily as she ended the call. Could she have inadvertently opened a new can of worms by suggesting that a murderer might be on the lam? Bronco had served his time, but what if he knew more than he admitted? And what if he had been guilty despite his insistence of his innocence?

THIRTY

Christie was tidying up the store as it neared closing time. A few minutes before five, Jason pulled up in front of the building and popped in through the door.

"Hey, Jason. Are you here to order flowers?"

"Hey, yourself. No, on the flowers. But I have a little more information for you."

Christie put her dust rag on the nearest counter and walked toward the front entrance. "What is it?"

"I found a few names from the bar fight in 1982. Mr. Thompson had another file with all the interviews he had done at the time. He had talked with the bartender, who was able to identify a half dozen of the men who were there in the bar when the fight broke out."

"Who were they?" Christie's eyes widened as she asked the question. "Did one of the names start with a 'B?'"

Jason shook his head and pulled a notepad from his coat pocket. "I knew you'd want the names, so I wrote them down. Tommy Jones, Jerry Ferguson, Martin Kugle, Rob Campbell,

Wes Knight, and Gordon McCready. No one with a first or last name starting with a 'B.' Sorry." He handed the list to Christie as she reached for it.

Christie scanned the list herself and furrowed her brow. "When I talked to Bronco earlier, he said there were a dozen or more men there, but most of them had scattered when they heard the siren. There are only six names here. What about the other men who were supposedly there?"

Jason shrugged. "Could have been men who happened to drop in and weren't regulars, so no one knew their names. Or they might have been buddies of the bartender who didn't want to get them in trouble for some reason. Or, I don't know."

Christie's shoulders sagged. "Or maybe Bronco lied and was the murderer after all. But he said he didn't write the note, so who's B?"

Jason put an arm around her shoulder. "It's just a note from a long time ago. It may not mean anything anymore. Why do you care so much about it?"

Christie shrugged off his arm. "I don't know. I suppose it's because of that guy dying after he got one of my floral arrangements and then the desk being stolen. And finding out there really was a girl named 'Missy' who has since disappeared."

"Can I cheer you up by taking you to dinner? It's 'Taco Thursday' at the Buzzard Bar tonight."

"Thanks, Jason. You're a doll, but I wouldn't be good company tonight, and I'm fixing you dinner tomorrow night anyway."

"Ah, so you haven't forgotten about that promise!"

"It might only be homemade tacos, but I will come up with something." Christie sniffled one last time and pocketed the tissue. "See you tomorrow night about six thirty."

Jason planted a small kiss on her forehead. He was six-foot-two compared to her five-foot-four. "I'll be there."

Christie closed and locked the door, waved at Jason as he turned back to blow her a kiss, and leaned against the door and sighed. Stormy had jumped down from her perch and rubbed her black fur against Christie's legs. She purred loudly when Christie picked her up and asked herself out loud, "Who was 'B'? I'm sure you would find some way to tell me if you could talk, wouldn't you, Stormy? Well, we'll probably never know. Let's go home."

CHRISTIE MADE herself a favorite quick meal of a toasted cheese sandwich and a handful of grapes. She figured it would count for a serving of dairy and fruit, plus fiber from the whole wheat bread.

Stormy had already curled up in Christie's favorite chair next to the fireplace by the time Christie had changed into comfy leggings and a sweatshirt. The cat stood up and stretched when her mistress scooted her over and sat down with a glass of merlot in hand, then promptly claimed possession of her lap.

Anita called while Christie was watching a recorded episode of one of the Hallmark shows. While she wasn't necessarily a huge fan of chick flicks, she was occasionally in the mood for something that guaranteed a happy ending.

"Hi, Anita. What's up?"

"I was just wondering if you'd made any progress with your mystery. You mentioned planning to call some businesses in Easton to try to locate the guy called Bronco."

"I'm not sure if you'd call it progress, but I located Teresa's parents. They still live in Centralia and answered at the phone number listed on her school application."

"That sounds like progress to me," exclaimed Anita.

"Mrs. Stewart confirmed that they called their daughter 'Missy' after having three busy boys but denied any knowledge of a note or a desk. She hung up on me after that, and I doubt she would welcome any more calls."

"So you didn't get a chance to ask where Teresa lives now?"

"In a word, no. And that's what I had hoped to find out. I may have gone about it wrong. Her tone of voice changed when I mentioned a murder."

"Maybe Jason's investigator will come up with something."

"Jason's coming over for dinner tomorrow evening, and I'm sure he'll tell me if he has learned anything new."

"Are you, like, dating?"

"I wouldn't call it that, but it's nice to have a tiny bit of a social life. I never developed one in the years I was in San Francisco."

Anita chuckled. "You can call it whatever you like, Christie, but it kinda sounds like dating to me."

Christie felt her face redden. "He's helping me solve my mystery, anyway. Today, he came by the shop with a list of six men who were in the bar the night of that fight and murder."

"Anyone promising?"

"No, and I talked to Bronco Carver today. He said he'd just stepped in to stop the fight but was the one holding the cue stick when the sheriff showed up. He said there were a dozen or more men in the bar during the fight, but they scattered. Some of them must have been caught in the parking lot, or maybe they were interviewed later. Jason said the bartender gave the sheriff a bunch of names of men who had been there."

"If there were a dozen men, and the bartender only named six of them, who were the others?"

"The bartender might not have known anyone except the locals. Someone like Bronco and his coworker were working in town and just dropped in for a beer. There were probably others like that."

"Let me know what you find out. And how your date goes with Jason tomorrow."

"It's not a date."

"Sounds like a date to me."

"Goodbye, Anita."

Christie ran her fingers through Stormy's soft black fur. "It's not a date, is it Stormy?"

THIRTY-ONE

Christie unlocked the back door of the shop and disarmed the alarm. She had a moment of panic every time she was the first one to open the door in the morning because she feared she would forget the combination or enter the wrong sequence and set off the alert. The security company had duly warned her that she was allowed three false alarms before being charged seventy-five dollars for future ones. So far, she and Aunt Doris had only goofed up once, and that was on Christie. She'd had transient number dyslexia and hadn't yet entered the number in her cell phone for backup. It was there now, however.

Her aunt had a doctor's appointment at nine o'clock, and Christie had cheerfully told her not to worry about the shop. She would be fine till noon, she thought, considering that there were no funerals on the calendar and no wedding on the schedule for Saturday. She hummed a song that had been on the radio during her short drive to the shop and even danced a few steps. She realized that she was looking forward to seeing

Jason that evening, although she wasn't ready to call it a date. She was simply repaying him for his investigative help.

Business was nonexistent for the first hour. She busied herself with dusting the shelves and rearranging the gift items until the first customers entered shortly after ten. She had just finished ringing up a purchase by Mrs. Princeton when she heard someone knock at the back door. Thinking it was her aunt who didn't want to get her key out, she jumped up and looked through the door's window before opening it. Heather was grinning and pointing to something out of Christie's sight.

"Hi, Heather," she said as she unlocked and opened the door. "How did your delivery go? Was there a problem?"

"No, no problems. They even gave me a tip. But I found something on my way to work. It's in my rig."

Christie popped out the door and went to Heather's SUV, which was sitting in the alley with the rear door open.

She shrieked when she saw Heather's cargo. "My desk! Where did you find it?"

"It was next to the Goodwill donation bin at the discount furniture shop on the other side of town. I stopped to look at it thinking it might be the one that was stolen. I wasn't sure it's the right one, but figured it was worth hauling it over here to show you."

"Did you ask about it at the furniture store before you took it?"

"Yes, and they said it wasn't theirs."

"It's definitely the one that was stolen from here. I recognize those drawer knobs," said Christie, glancing at the drawers which lay on the mat next to the desk. "Let's get it inside." She helped Heather pull it out of the vehicle and carry it into the shop.

Christie checked it over while Heather went back outside to retrieve the drawers.

"I don't see any major damage," Christie announced once the six small drawers were back in place. "It's a good thing it didn't rain last night."

Heather said, "The little drawers were all pulled out when I first got there, so I just left them that way. I figured they might fall out anyway when I was driving."

Christie hugged Heather. "Thank you. I'm just glad to have it back. I need to call Chief Conway and let him know where you found it so he can clarify that you were recovering stolen property. I don't want anyone to think I was stealing a donation to Goodwill."

"Do you think he'll check it for fingerprints like they do on all those television shows?" Heather wiggled an eyebrow.

"Maybe, but he'll have to make that decision." Christie stepped back, her right elbow in her left hand as she surveyed the desk. "I guess whoever took it didn't really want it after all if it was the note they were hoping to find."

"I gotta run back to school, Christie. I used my free period to deliver this, and I don't want to be late."

"Of course, but wait one sec." Christie retrieved her purse from the back room, handed Heather a twenty and hugged her again. "Thank you, young lady. You made my day."

CHIEF CONWAY WAS at Christie's shop within fifteen minutes of her call.

"Are you absolutely sure this is the same desk?" he asked. He looked at it more closely. "I remember my grandmother having one like this when I was a kid. We used to play 'Post Office' with it and put letters in the drawers." He chuckled.

"Yes, I'm sure. If you look at the knobs on the upper drawers, you'll notice that one is different from the other five."

Christie pointed out the odd knob, which was dull brass with a flat face, whereas the others were all rounded and shiny. "I noticed that when I was cleaning it up for sale."

"It's probably pointless to dust for fingerprints, but I'll do it anyway, just to be thorough." Conway opened a small box with a brush and powder. "It won't take long if you want to take care of your customers."

"Sure. Thank you." Christie went to the counter to ring up a couple of items for an older woman she recognized from the church she had attended as a youngster. "Hello, Mrs. Murphy. Did you find everything you wanted today?"

"Yes, I did, Christie. You've done a great job of spiffing up your grandmother's shop. Nice and modern now. I'll be stopping by regularly now that I know what you have in here."

"Why, thank you. That's wonderful. Do you need these gift wrapped today?"

"Oh, that would be nice. My arthritic fingers don't do that as well as they used to. This is a birthday gift for my best friend, Clara."

"Fabulous choice. I'm sure she'll love it." Christie placed the figurine in a small box and expertly wrapped it with a happy floral print paper. Having noticed the birthday card's yellow envelope, she used a coordinating yellow ribbon for the bow and trim. "Here you go. Thanks for coming in."

Christie answered some questions about taking care of cut flowers for a woman who had selected a fresh bouquet from the refrigerated cooler. She had just finished ringing up the sale when she heard Conway say, "I'm done."

"That was fast," said Christie. "How soon will you get results?"

"Not for a few days, I'm afraid. There were mostly a lot of smudges, but I did manage to find a few isolated prints."

"Those might be mine or Heather's," admitted Christie.

"But I'll keep my fingers crossed that our bad guy wasn't very smart and left a few of his own."

CHAPTER

THIRTY-TWO

The shop was moderately busy in the afternoon, perhaps because the sun had broken through the November gloom, creating an opportunity for shoppers to venture outdoors without getting wet. Christie dismissed her aunt an hour early after promising to finish the floral arrangements that were going to be picked up the next day.

Because she was busy helping customers, the time flew by, and it was five o'clock before Christie knew it. She locked the front door, scooped up Stormy, and headed out after setting the alarm. She had picked up groceries for the meal she was preparing for Jason the evening before. She had even done some of the prepping — she'd cut up the broccoli, bell peppers, onion and chicken — so she could prepare the main course more quickly once her guest arrived.

After feeding her kitty and starting the rice, she had just enough time to change clothes and freshen her makeup. She stood in front of her closet and considered several options before settling on taupe jeans, a heather-pink, long-sleeved

Tee and short boots. Casual and comfortable, yet a little more upscale than the khaki pants and long-sleeved shirt she'd worn to work.

Christie felt as though her heart were racing, but her pulse was slow and steady when she checked her wrist. Nerves, she decided...even though it wasn't a date. Stormy had agreed with her. Christie jumped when she heard the doorbell and took a big breath before putting on a smile and opening the door. She laughed when she saw Jason standing in the door with a bouquet of flowers.

"Flowers? How special!" She gave him a little kiss on the cheek as he entered and handed them to her. "I'll find a vase."

"I hope it's okay that I got them at Trader Joe's. It seemed awkward to buy them at your shop. That would have spoiled the surprise." He shed his coat while she put water in a gold-colored vase and added the flowers.

"I think it's very thoughtful of you, Jason. Thank you."

Christie placed the vase on her dining table and said, "Follow me into the kitchen. I'm making a stir-fry, and it has to be done at the last minute or it gets soggy. You can open that bottle of wine on the counter and pour a couple of glasses while I get started on the chicken."

"Cheers," said Jason as he handed Christie a glass of Riesling a few minutes later. She winked in response and clinked his glass.

"Would you like to know about Brian Stone first? Or Lynette?"

"Both!"

"You can't have both at once. You have to choose."

"Okay. Then start with Lynette since she's been around recently."

"Good choice."

"Huh?"

"Wine, I mean, not Lynette. So, it turns out she was born in Spokane, adopted by a young attorney and his wife, and got a bachelor's degree in sociology at Whitman College."

"Oh, so she could be the baby Missy gave up for adoption when she went to Spokane! Finally, some pieces come together."

Jason nodded. "My investigator believes she's Teresa Stewart's daughter."

"You're kidding," said Christie as she added the chicken to the hot oil in the wok. "Do you think Teresa knows about her daughter's current life?"

"Not sure. Les, the investigator, is still working on that. He's looking for emails and that sort of thing. He said it was a closed adoption, as most were forty years ago. Not as many were open adoptions then."

"And she may not have wanted any of her friends to know. But Teresa went to Spokane to live with relatives, didn't she? They would have known she had a baby, I would think."

"Probably, but if it was a closed adoption, they wouldn't know any other details."

"At any rate, considering her adoptive parents, it suggests that she was raised in a relatively affluent family, considering that Whitman is a private university and her father was an attorney."

"I agree." Jason leaned his nose closer to the wok. "That's smelling really good."

Christie finished sautéing the chicken and added the vegetables to the pan. "What else do you know?"

"She spent a gap year in France, and when she came back, she went back to school and got a Master's degree in social work."

"That's admirable." Christie added broccoli florets and red bell pepper strips to the carrots and onion. "I had a cousin who was a case worker for Child Protective Services. She said it broke her heart to see how some of her clients treated their children. One couple fed their three-year-old daughter dog food, but their older children had normal human food. Disgusting. Sorry for interrupting. Go on."

"I've heard stories like that myself. Anyway, she started her career in Spokane but transferred to Olympia a couple of years ago. She's still working as a caseworker but is mostly in management at the state level."

"Hmm. I wonder if Lynette did some research, considering the kind of work she does, and traced her birth mother to White Castle," said Christie as she checked the rice and deemed it perfectly cooked.

Jason nodded and refilled their empty wine glasses while Christie dished up the rice and stir-fry into serving dishes.

"Time to eat, Mr. Princeton."

They spent the next few minutes enjoying the delicious meal while watching Stormy play with a catnip mouse.

"I wonder if the phrase about 'cat and mouse' came about because of catnip-infused mice," said Jason.

"I'm quite sure that's not the original meaning, but Stormy is always the winner in her version of the game. I'd feel sorry for the mouse if it were real."

Jason laughed as he visualized Stormy playing with a real mouse. "Are you ready to hear about Brian Stone?"

"Please! Do you know where he is?"

Jason leaned back in his chair, sated by the food and wine. "Turns out he never went far from his hometown. He's worked in construction most of the time. Got started with his father's business and went out on his own about twenty years ago after his father died."

"Is he married? Does he have children?"

"Never married as far as Les could determine. Presumably, no children."

"Have you talked with him?"

"No, but I have an address and a phone number if you want to contact him."

Christie jumped up from her chair and gave Jason a big hug. "Of course, I want to contact him. Wasn't he from Adna?"

"Yes, but he lives in Easton now."

"Easton? That's where Bronco Carver worked for the Lewis County PUD. Do you suppose they've stayed in touch?"

"It's a smallish town," said Jason. "It's bigger than White Castle, but it wouldn't surprise me to find out they run into each other on occasion."

Christie began to clear the table. Jason stood up to help, saying, "My mom taught me how to help in the kitchen." He put his arms around her and said, "That was a great meal."

Christie felt her face redden as she smiled. "Thanks. I'm glad you liked it."

"Do you want to call this Brian guy when we're done with the dishes?"

"Absolutely. I'm dying to hear the rest of his story."

"I'm not sure what I should say," said Christie. "What if it's a wrong number? What if he doesn't want to talk about that night? What if he hangs up on me?"

Jason laughed and clasped her hands in his. "Just dial the number and play it by ear. Tell him the truth. That's all I would want if you were calling me."

"That didn't go so well when I talked with Missy's parents, but I'll do it." Christie took a big breath and picked up her cell.

"Here goes. Wish me luck." She tapped the green phone icon after entering the ten digits.

Jason responded with a wink.

"This is Brian."

Christie first thought she was listening to the start of a recording but a split second later realized that Brian was waiting for someone to talk. "Hi, Brian. You don't know me. My name is Christie O'Mara from White Castle, and I am calling about an incident forty years ago at a local bar."

Brian didn't say anything for a few seconds. He finally said, "What about it?"

Christie's shoulders relaxed, and she caught Jason's eye. "Do you remember a young student teacher at White Castle High School called 'Missy?'"

"Why do you want to know? That was a long time ago."

"It's a long story, and I'd love to tell you more about it if you're the young man who wrote a note to her."

"I wrote a few notes to her, but I'm not sure what you're talking about."

Christie paused, took a breath, and said, "I found a note from someone signing as 'B' to Missy. It mentioned something about a possible murder."

"Where did you find it?"

"Are you saying that you did write a note like that?"

"What does it matter now? That was forty years ago. I got over her. I moved on."

"It could matter a lot, but I don't want to tell you over the phone. Would you be willing to meet me somewhere? I can tell you what I've discovered and you can decide what, if anything, you want to do about it."

"Are you a reporter or something? Or involved with the police?"

"Neither of those. I'm a normal person with a curious

nature and a strong sense of justice." Christie chewed on her lip.

Brian was quiet for a moment. Finally, he said, "There's a McMenamin's Olympic Pub on Tower Road in Centralia. It's about halfway between here and White Castle. Are you able to meet me there tomorrow at about one o'clock?"

Christie's heart quickened. "Yes, I'll be there. Is it okay with you if I bring a friend?"

"Sure."

"See you then."

Christie held her phone to her chest for a moment. She turned to Jason. "He's going to meet me in Centralia tomorrow. Will you go with me? I don't think he's a murderer, but I would feel safer with you riding shotgun."

Jason chuckled. "It sounds odd that you would use the words 'murderer' and 'shotgun' in the same sentence in this situation."

They both laughed at the incongruent choice of words and drank more wine.

THIRTY-THREE

The morning hours at the flower shop seemed to drag. A few women bought cards and gifts for a baby shower. A group of teenage girls wandered around and laughed at the napkins with funny sayings but left without making a purchase. Just before noon, Christie saw Jason pull into a parking space across the street. She put on her best smile and waited for him to enter the shop before going to retrieve her jacket from the back room.

"Auntie Doris," she said as she shrugged on the jacket. "Jason's here, and we're going to head up to Centralia to meet the mysterious Brian."

Doris looked up from the tabletop arrangement of purple, pink and white flowers she was working on. "You be careful, young lady. Don't get yourself into hot water over this."

Christie threw her arms around her aunt and hugged her. "Thank you. I've got Jason to keep me safe. Thanks for taking care of the store this afternoon. I'll owe you."

Christie grabbed her tote on the way to the door where Jason stood, hands in the pockets of his warm overcoat. She turned and blew a kiss to her aunt as she exited. Doris shook her head.

The thirty miles from White Castle to Centralia felt like a longer drive than it was. Christie was anxious and worried and excited. She wasn't sure which emotion was strongest. She practiced a few opening words with Jason but finally gave up when she realized she would just have to trust herself to say what needed to be said when she met Brian face to face.

Christie read about the McMenamins Olympic Club Pub on the website as Jason cruised up the freeway. The pub occupied the former card room of the Olympic Club Hotel & Theater, where the likes of Tacoma Iron Mike, Honest John and One-Eyed Tony once convened nightly for spirited games of poker.

She told Jason, "Some friends of mine stayed there a few years back and were told that some of the rooms were reserved for 'ladies of the night' who entertained the men coming home from the logging camps. There was even an escaped train robber, Roy Gardner, who stayed there a few nights until he was caught."

Jason replied, "I've heard things like that happened frequently a hundred years ago." He pulled up in front of the old building. "Here we are, Christie. Are you ready?"

She took a big breath. "Yes, I am. Let's go find out the rest of the story about the note."

Jason and Christie entered the Pub. They stood for a couple of minutes, taking in the splendor of the dark wood, Art Nouveau stenciling, Tiffany-style lights, beveled glass and one of the most beautiful period bars imaginable. They peeked into the classically styled pool room, which housed seven original Brunswick pool tables. When they turned around, Christie saw a distinguished-looking man with black hair touched with silver sitting alone at a table near a huge wood stove.

He caught her eye, nodded and stood. Christie returned the nod, took Jason's hand, and led the way to the table.

"You must be Brian Stone," she said, offering her hand. "I'm Christie O'Mara, and this is my friend, Jason Princeton."

"Pleased to meet you," said Brian, with a handshake of his own.

After everyone was seated, Brian said, "I almost changed my mind about coming, but your comments about that note brought back a lot of memories."

"I hope some of them were good," said Christie.

"Yes," he said, smiling. "They were good until that night at the bar when a fight broke out, and I felt I had to leave town."

"Will you tell me about it?" asked Christie. "I read some newspaper articles about it, but I'd love to hear it from your point of view."

Brian waited to answer until after the waiter took orders for coffee and water all around.

"My friend, Bronco, and I..."

"Bronco Carver?" Christie interrupted.

"Yes, Bronco Carver. He and another buddy from work and I stopped by the bar after work before heading back up to Adna. It was a normal crowd of guys from the woods or from the mills, all having a beer or two before heading home. You know what I mean?"

Christie and Jason nodded.

"All of a sudden, some guy that I didn't know started yelling about staying away from his friend." Brian shook his head, looking down at the table. "I didn't think he was talking to me, but he grabbed a cue stick and started hitting me with it. So someone handed one to me, and I used it like I was fencing him and defending myself with it. Bronco and other guys jumped into the fight and were trying to defend me. Some had cue sticks, and some used their fists."

"Then I heard sirens, and most of the guys scattered. I think Bronco grabbed the stick from the dude who was yelling at me. I guess that guy got out the back door like I did. I felt really bad when I heard that Bronco got caught and ended up with jail time. The guy who died had been hit accidentally when the crazy man started swatting at me. I guess he was just in the way."

"Did you ever find out who was cussing at you? The one who started the fight, I mean," asked Christie.

"No. I didn't know him, and at the time, I just wanted to get out of there. I knew Bronco was innocent, but nobody believed him except the defense attorney, I guess, even though at least one other person testified on his behalf at the trial. So I quit my job and went into the army and did my four years. When I got out I went to Adna first, then ended up in Easton. And that's the end of the story."

"Did you ever consider talking with Bronco's attorney about offering testimony when you got out of the army and found out what had happened?"

"Yeah, I called his office once and he said he needed more than my word against the sheriff's. And I didn't have anything else to offer. Bronco told me when we met up a few years back that the evidence of him holding the cue stick was considered too strong against anyone's word. And the sheriff was adamant that Bronco was guilty."

"What about the note that you wrote to Missy?" asked Christie. "How did it end up in the desk at my shop?"

"I wouldn't know about a desk," he replied with a puzzled look. "Once I decided to leave, I stopped at the twenty-four-hour coffee shop at the end of town and gave a note for Missy to one of the waitresses. She promised to get it to her when I told her the situation."

"Did she know who Missy was?"

"Sure did. Missy and I used to stop there and have coffee and pastry on Sunday afternoons when she got back into town."

Christie held the warm coffee mug in her hands and said, "Hmm. So how did it get in that desk?"

Brian reiterated. "What desk?"

THIRTY-FOUR

Christie cocked her head, eyes narrowed, looking at Brian. "The writing desk that I found in my grandmother's flower shop. When I was cleaning it up for sale, I found an envelope with a note taped to the bottom of one of the drawers. It was written to 'Missy' and signed 'B.'" Christie scrolled her phone to the photo she'd taken of it and passed it to Brian. "Did you write this note?"

Brian nodded slowly and returned the phone. "I did, but I don't know anything about a desk."

"Hmm. That's interesting," said Christie. "I originally thought the desk might have come from Missy's home, but now I realize that wouldn't make sense because you two were dating in White Castle. Is that right?"

"Yeah. I never went to her parents' home in Centralia. She lived in White Castle with a local family and went home most weekends. So did I, so we mostly went to the movies or out for dinner on weeknights."

"Did you see her again after that night?"

Brian shook his head, his lips pinched. "No. I hoped I

would hear from her through the coffee shop before I left for the army. We used to leave each other messages there with Sandra, the evening waitress, so I checked a few times over the next few weeks. Sandra told me she didn't see or hear from Missy again. When I called the school, they said she'd left several weeks before the end of the school year and didn't leave a forwarding address or number. The office gave me her parents' number and I tried calling them, but they hung up on me as soon as I said my name."

Christie probed, "I was confused because the note was written on a piece of paper with an M at the top, like someone's personal stationery. Who was 'M?'"

"My mother's name is Margaret. Once when I'd gone home she'd given me some of her notepaper when I didn't have anything to write on."

"Well, that solves one little mystery," said Christie. "Did you know Missy was pregnant?"

Brian's face went ashen. He covered his eyes with his hand and looked down, his elbow resting on the table. When he finally looked up again, he said, "No wonder her parents wouldn't talk to me. But they didn't tell me. And neither did Missy, obviously. But how do *you* know?"

Christie looked at Jason as if for permission to tell Brian more of the story. Jason nodded, so she went on and explained how she had searched the old newspapers for an event that fit the few details in the note and found news articles about the cue stick murder. She had learned Missy's real name, Teresa Stewart, from her parents' neighbor, Jack Smith, who had lived in town all his life. Her high school English teacher had told her she'd thought Missy might be pregnant, which was still a relative taboo in the early eighties despite Missy being in her early twenties. Then Jason offered to help and asked his private investigator to try to find Missy, Bronco and Brian.

"The search for Missy revealed that she'd gone to Spokane, where she had an aunt and uncle, then had a child, a girl, which she gave up for adoption. The daughter taught school there for a while, but Les, the investigator, hasn't been able to trace her any further as of yet."

Brian's eyes remained wide as he listened to Christie continue, "This is only a hunch, but a strong one, that her daughter — possibly *your* daughter — might be a young woman named Lynette Nichols. She works in Olympia for the Department of Social and Health Services. She showed up at my flower shop in White Castle about a week ago, but I haven't seen her since."

"Are you thinking she traced us, her birth parents, back to White Castle?" Brian asked.

"Possibly, especially if Missy didn't want her parents to know about it. When she had the baby, she might have used the address of the couple she had been living with while student teaching."

"Of course. That makes sense. But why didn't she tell me?" Brian's eyes welled with tears. "I would have married her and taken care of her."

Christie said kindly, "Maybe she never got your note. You mentioned that the waitress said she never saw Missy again, right? And you went into the army. How could she have found you?"

Brian was quiet, both elbows on the table, chin in his hands. He asked Jason, "Are you still looking for her?"

"I am," Jason replied. "I was planning to have my PI call Lynnette, her daughter— or at least the woman we believe to be her daughter. Her last known workplace was in Olympia. You might have better luck than me with a phone call. I'll forward the report to your phone if you want to contact her instead."

Brian and Jason exchanged cell numbers while Christie added French vanilla creamer to her fresh mug of coffee.

"Will you let me know what you find out?" asked Christie. She suddenly sat up straight. "Oh, I just had a thought, but it's a shot in the dark."

"What's that?" Brian asked. "I'll try a shot in the dark if it helps find Missy."

"What if we could find Sandra, the waitress at the coffee shop? That note must have left her hands somehow, in order for it to end up in the desk. Perhaps she gave it to someone to deliver to Missy when Missy didn't show up again? And if she did, who was it?"

"We can stop there when we get back to White Castle," said Jason. "Depending on her age when this all happened, she could very well still be alive. And might still be living in the area."

"I'd say she was in her thirties or early forties back then," offered Brian. "I remember her saying she had two kids in their early teens and that she wanted to put them in boxes and keep them there till they grew up." He managed a smile. "She was kidding, of course, but she said it in all seriousness."

Christie said, "We'll do our best to find her. She's our best link to find out where the note went next. And maybe *that* person is who taped it to the underside of the desk drawer."

THIRTY-FIVE

JoJo's Coffee Shop at Exit 49 had been a fixture in the community for fifty years or more. Christie remembered stopping there now and then after shopping with her mother. Freshly baked maple bars had been her favorite pastry back then and were still a special treat.

Jason held the door open for her. She looked at him and asked, "What if she's dead? What if she's alive but doesn't remember?"

Jason gave a slight nod. "Let's ask. I have a good feeling about it."

Christie took a big breath and led the way to the counter. A young woman with bright magenta hair and tattoos covering her left arm greeted her. Her name tag read "Sierra."

Sierra smiled and said, "Hi. What can I get for you?"

"I don't need anything to eat, thank you. I realize this is a long shot, but I'm here to ask about a waitress named Sandra who used to work here."

"I don't know her myself, but I'll ask the owner. She's in the back finishing a batch of maple bars."

Christie's mouth watered. "I love maple bars! I'll take a couple when they're ready!"

"Sure. Just give me a minute."

Christie crossed her fingers and chewed her lip. Jason's hand rested on her shoulder.

A woman who appeared to be in her sixties came out from a door behind the display case. She placed a tray of maple bars on a table behind Sierra and wiped her flour-covered hands on her apron. The black chef's apron already displayed evidence of the pastries she had been creating during the day. Her hair was kept out of the way with a floral cap, but wisps of gray peeked out along her temples.

She wiped the perspiration from her brow with a towel that had been lying on the counter and said, "Hi. I'm Louise. Sierra said you asked about Sandra. What would you like to know?"

Christie's heart skipped a beat. "Do you know where she is? I'd love to talk to her about something that happened about forty years ago."

"Ooh. That's a while back. Can you tell me what it's about?"

Christie paused. "I doubt anyone else would know about it. It was a small thing — just a note from a man to a woman."

Louise's face lit up. "Well, young lady, you're in luck. Sandra's my aunt. I bought the business from her about twenty years ago, but she can't stay away. She still comes in and helps me out occasionally when I need her."

Christie caught her breath. "Do you think I could talk to her?"

Louise picked up a pen and wrote something on a sticky note. "She lives at the beach now in Ocean Park. Here's her phone number. Go ahead and give her a call. Tell her I gave you the number. And please come back and tell me what happens."

"Absolutely, if you'll let me buy a half dozen of those maple bars."

Once back in the car, Christie turned to Jason and said, "Let's share these maple bars. I know my mom and dad love them, and your parents might enjoy them as well."

"Great idea. What about Sandra? Aren't you going to call her?" he asked as he started the engine and prepared to leave the parking area.

Christie shivered, but not because she felt cold. "I'm not sure what to say to her."

"She's either going to remember the note or not. Just ask her."

Christie straightened her shoulders and swallowed. "Okay. Here goes." She tapped in the number and closed her eyes. One ring. Two rings. Three rings. "She's not answering."

"Then leave a message."

One more ring. Then, instead of a recorded voice, Christie heard a breathless "Hello?"

"Sandra?"

"Yes, this is Sandra. Who's calling?"

"Christie. Christie O'Mara from the flower shop in White Castle."

"Maude's granddaughter?"

"Yes. Exactly. I'm so glad to reach you."

"I remember you coming in now and then with your mother. So, how can I help you?

"First, I'm supposed to tell you I got your number from your niece Louise at JoJo's. She said it would be okay for me to call you. Second, for the reason I called, do you remember a handwritten note that Brian Stone gave to you about forty years ago to give to Missy Stewart?"

"Oh, my goodness. That was a long time ago. Let me think for a second."

Christie found herself holding her breath, waiting for Sandra to say something.

"Brian Stone. He was working construction on the highway project if I remember correctly, and he came in for coffee almost every day."

"Yes, and he was dating Missy. Do you remember that?"

"I only saw her a couple of times when I worked swing shift, but he talked a lot about her." She chuckled. "I think he was in love…"

"Did he give you a note to pass on to her?"

"Yes, I remember because I left it on the counter next to the register, thinking she would come by to get it. She never did, at least not that I saw, so after a couple of weeks, I gave it to one of the other regulars who said he knew her and would deliver it himself."

"Who was that?"

"You would ask, wouldn't you? That was such a long time ago, and my memory isn't as good as it used to be, except when I'm baking at JoJo's. I can remember all those recipes just fine. Golly — I just can't remember which one of the men it was. I'm sorry."

"That's okay. I knew there was a chance you wouldn't remember."

"Why do you need to know, if I may ask?"

"Do you remember the fight at the bar up the highway from JoJo's about forty years ago where someone died after he was attacked by a cue stick?"

"Of course! That was the talk of the town for weeks afterward, and so was the murder trial. None of us knew the man who got convicted. He was one of those construction workers, too, I guess. So how is Brian Stone connected to that?"

"He was at the bar that night and left town afterward. I guess you could say he was a witness. But I'm just trying to find out how that note ended up taped to a desk drawer that ended up in my grandmother's flower shop."

"Gee, I sure can't help you with that. You know, sometimes I remember things later after my brain has had a chance to think on it. May I call you if that happens?"

"Please, yes. That would be great." Christie shared her phone number, followed by a promise to tell her mother "hello" for Sandra.

"She doesn't remember who she gave the note to," said Christie. "Back to square one, I guess."

Jason reached over and patted her leg. "Don't give up. She'll probably remember tomorrow when she takes her morning shower. Like the rest of us."

THIRTY-SIX

Christie called Anita as soon as she got home. She'd turned down a dinner invite from Jason because she didn't feel like making small talk after coming up empty on the phone call to Sandra.

"You spent the day with Jason? What were you doing?"

Christie shared details of the day about having met Brian, the writer of the note, and talking on the phone with Sandra, who had worked at JoJo's.

"The JoJo's here in town? Does she still work there?"

"No. She sold the shop to her niece and lives at the beach, but she still comes in and bakes sometimes. Brian had left the note with her to give to Missy, but Sandra said she never saw her again. And that she gave the note to someone else to deliver."

"Who did she give it to?"

"She couldn't remember," said Christie with a sigh. "I was so close! But she said she'll call me if it comes to her later."

Anita commiserated. "Maybe she'll remember in the shower like I do."

Christie laughed. "That's the same thing Jason said!"

"Well, it's true. Do you want to do something tomorrow? We both have the day off."

"Yeah, but it's going to be cold and rainy according to the forecast. How about coming over and we can make cookies like we used to do? I can take some to the flower shop, and your fellow teachers would love to find fresh cookies in the teachers' lounge."

"Great idea. Is one thirty good? That'll give me enough time in the morning to finish grading essays."

"And I'll finish the orders for the shop. See you tomorrow."

Christie rummaged in the fridge till she found Chinese leftovers that were still edible. That and a mug of hot buttered rum warmed her soul while she scanned email messages. Stormy joined her in her grandmother's armchair when she sat down to watch a Hallmark movie. Even though they all followed the same plot, Christie enjoyed them when she was in the right mood. Maybe because they always had a happy ending. And she wanted one of those for Brian and Missy and Lynette.

Halfway through the program, her phone buzzed in her pocket. She didn't recognize the number. Christie muted the television and pressed the green icon. "Hello. Christie here."

"This is your old neighbor, Jack. I hope it's not too late to call."

"No, not at all. How can I help you? The shop is closed if you're calling about flowers."

"No, not tonight. I was wondering if you had figured out any more about that bar fight you asked me about."

"A little bit. My friend Jason found out that Bronco Carver, the guy who was convicted for the killing of Arnold Youngman, is still alive and working in Easton."

"He is? Didn't he go to jail?"

"Yes, but he did his time. We talked to him, and he told us he was innocent. The actual guilty party was never identified according to what he told me."

"He can't admit it, huh? He was found guilty, fair and square. I was there."

"What do you mean? Oh, yeah. Your dad was deputy sheriff back then, wasn't he?" She had forgotten, and now she was basically telling her neighbor that his father had failed at his job. She shook her head, wishing she'd think ahead a bit more before talking to people. She tried to veer the subject a bit with, "Did you go to a lot of trials when you were young?"

"No, just that one. Well, I won't keep you. Will you let me know if you ever figure out the rest of the story?"

"Sure. Have a good evening, Jack."

Christie stared at the phone for a moment, puzzled by Jack's call. She shrugged and ran her fingers through Stormy's thick hair. "I wonder what he really wanted to know," she asked her cat. Stormy stretched, rearranged herself on the blanket, and started purring.

The Hallmark movie ended predictably with the young man convincing the young woman that he was earnest in his caring for her and they were destined to live happily ever after. Christie smiled to herself. Only in fairy tales and Hallmark movies did that happen. But not always in fairy tales as they were told in their original European versions. She had read enough of them in an English literature class to learn that they were not the same as the sanitized versions of the children's stories she'd read growing up. "Even fairy tales are a sham," she said to Stormy.

THIRTY-SEVEN

The morning weather was as dark and rainy as the weatherman had predicted. Christie was grateful for a warm house with a fire and a good roof. She puttered in the kitchen, pulling out the ingredients for both oatmeal raisin and snickerdoodle cookies — two of her favorites. She would have Anita make one variety, and she would make the other. They'd have twice the number of cookies in less time than usual, although she'd have to allow extra time for baking.

A thunderstorm with lightning and thunder passed through the neighborhood shortly after noon. Her lights flicked off and back on a couple of times. Christie crossed her fingers that she would have power during her cookie-baking session. The rain was still coming down in buckets when Anita rang the doorbell.

"That's a lot of rain," said her friend, shaking her umbrella before leaving it fully open to dry. "I'm glad I don't have a basement right about now. My parents used to have to keep a pair of sump pumps going in weather like this. I swore I'd never have a basement because of growing up with that experience."

"I'll take your coat," said Christie. "It is nasty outside, but so far, my power has stayed on. And I don't have a basement to worry about."

Christie poured a couple of glasses of cabernet sauvignon and invited Anita to sit in the family room and chat for a bit before starting the cookie factory.

"This fire is so comfortable," said Anita. "I'll bet Stormy sleeps in here a lot. I know I would." She patted the arms of the chair.

"She does indeed. She'll come and check on me every now and then if I'm not in here with her, but she always returns to her cozy bed where she is right now. I suppose she's making sure I'm okay."

"Tell me more about yesterday — about Jason, I mean. Do you see him as dating material?"

Christie furrowed her brow, thinking. "Maybe, but I'm not sure he's the man I'd want to marry."

"But isn't it nice to have someone to go out with on a date now and then? That's one of the disadvantages of a small town: not enough eligible men."

Christie chuckled. "Well, I didn't see many of them around when I lived in San Francisco either."

The girls laughed and shared a couple of man-stories, then Christie said, "Speaking of men, I got a call from Jack Smith last night."

"Jack Smith, as in the deputy sheriff's son? Why would he call you? He's way too old!"

"That's the one, but it wasn't about wanting to go on a date. He was curious if I had learned any more about that bar fight. A week ago, I'd asked him about it because Aunt Doris thought he might recall more than she did. He said then that he didn't."

"What did you tell him?"

"I only told him that I'd talked to Bronco Carver and how he swore he was innocent. Jack said Bronco was definitely guilty regardless of what he said. After his reaction, my sixth sense told me to be careful not to say anything more. He'd even gone to the trial."

"Wasn't he in his twenties back then? What normal twenty-something guy goes to a murder trial? Or maybe he followed trials because of his father?"

"That's what I thought. But he said that was the only one he attended." Christie stood up and tilted her head toward the kitchen. "We'd better get to work on our project."

A couple of hours later, while the last of the ten trays of cookies cooled enough to pack into containers, Christie and Anita enjoyed a second glass of wine in front of the fire. "Have you given up on finding your 'Missy?' It certainly seems like she doesn't want to be found."

"She might not know anyone's looking for her," said Christie. "It sounds like she never knew about the note. She probably gave up on Brian many years ago."

"Nowadays, adopted children often search for their parents," replied Anita. "I wonder if she's worried her daughter will find her."

Christie said soberly, "Or maybe she's afraid she won't."

They were both quiet for a few minutes, the only sounds being the crackle of the fire and the ticking of the grandfather clock in the corner of the comfortable room.

"I wonder if Missy's parents would be more willing to talk with me if I showed up at the door," Christie suggested, "instead of trying to call them again. They might know where she is."

"Yeah. It's hard to believe they would abandon their daughter forever."

"Well, they could have some religious beliefs that prevent them from forgiving her. Maybe they had a big falling-out when this all happened and they're still waiting for their daughter to contact them."

"Didn't you say she had some brothers? What if you were able to track down one of them?"

Christie sat up straight. "Anita, that's a great idea! I never even thought about trying to go through a back door to locate Missy. Of course, I need to get contact information and then see if any of them will talk to me and if they know anything."

"That's probably better than getting a door slammed in your face if you try to visit the parents."

"Let's package up the cookies. Then I'll call Jason and see if he's willing to help with one more thing."

THIRTY-EIGHT

Jason promised to have Les track down the Stewart brothers in exchange for home-baked cookies, which Christie delivered in person at his office the next morning. This was the first time she would be trying her later Monday morning opening time at eleven. So far, she enjoyed having the extra time to run errands such as this. She planned to spend the rest of her freed-up time spiffing up her shop and readying it for the next holiday, Veterans' Day, which was right around the corner.

She'd found her grandmother's stash of decorations in a banker's box in the storage room the previous week. Some of them were too dingy and sorry-looking to be used, and others were damaged. She was delighted to find that there were enough small American flags to create a display for the main counter. She'd asked Aunt Doris to make a few patriotic decorations from red, white and blue ribbons, and she scattered them around the shop. The total effect was just the right touch for the special day that was squeezed in between Halloween and Thanksgiving. She'd been proud of her own relatives serving in the military and wanted to pay all servicemen and -women a bit of homage.

"These snickerdoodles are delicious," pronounced Aunt Doris when she came in a little later. "I might eat all of them myself." She winked at her niece. "Are you going to have fresh-baked cookies in the shop on a regular basis?"

"That's not a bad idea," said Christie. "I enjoy baking, and it might bring in customers once word gets out."

"I'm all about advertising," replied her aunt. "Your cat won't get into them, will she?"

"I brought a glass cover to keep them a little fresher. It'll keep Stormy from trying to steal one, as well as help to keep other little fingers out." Christie grinned.

Christie shared the news about finding Brian Stone, who acknowledged he had written the note, and about talking to Sandra, the waitress at JoJo's. "She remembered Brian leaving the note with her to give to Missy but couldn't recall to whom she'd given it when Missy didn't come in to claim it after a couple of weeks. It seems that Missy never knew about it."

"Communication was a lot different back then," said her aunt. "If we'd had cell phones and email, there wouldn't be a reason to leave a note at a coffee shop."

"And there wasn't any way for Brian to let Missy know he'd left the note. He never said if he knew the name of the family where she stayed, and he said her parents hung up on him when he tried calling them directly."

"What are you going to do next, Christie?"

Christie munched on a cookie. "I asked Jason if he would track down Missy's brothers. She had three of them, all older. I hope one of them has stayed in touch with her, even if she was denounced by her parents."

"That's certainly a possibility, especially if she was close to one of them."

"I bribed him with a plate of cookies." Christie giggled and snitched an oatmeal raisin cookie for herself.

"The way to a man's heart is through his stomach, you know."

"I'm not trying to get to his heart," Christie protested. "Just his investigative skills."

"Of course." Aunt Doris started whistling.

The conversation was interrupted by the chime of the front door. A couple of women from Christie's parents' church entered and started browsing.

"Good morning, ladies. We have fresh cookies and coffee next to the counter if you're hungry."

Christie busied herself with the flower and greenery order that had arrived earlier. She noticed that the number of stems she was ordering was trending upwards, albeit she had only been open two full weeks. She took that as a good sign.

She knew from her experience of working with her grandmother during her younger years that the flower business was slow during November until orders for Thanksgiving center-pieces and cornucopias began, thus starting the holiday floral season. Of course, there would always be the random funeral plus requests for bouquets for anniversaries and birthdays.

Once December rolled around, she expected that the biggest money would come from table decorations for banquets and parties and perhaps a few holiday wreaths for doors. There was always the high school Christmas dance as well for which she would be creating boutonnieres and corsages for the local teens.

She was snapped back to reality when the women approached the register. Each of them had selected several cards and gift items. While Christie rang up their purchases, they enjoyed their coffee and cookies.

"What a nice idea," said the woman wearing a black raincoat. She nibbled on a snickerdoodle. "And this cookie is perfect."

The second woman, wearing a red anorak with her black jeans, agreed. "I might come back just for the cookies."

Everyone laughed. When they were gone, Christie said to her aunt, "I think I'll bake cookies for the shop on Sunday afternoons. I can make enough for the week and keep them in the freezer so they'll be fresh the whole week."

"Or you could have them only on a certain day of the week and make that a special day of some kind. You wouldn't have to bake so many that way."

"Which day do you think it should be, Auntie?"

"Well, it could be the lightest day and see if it brings in traffic, or it could be the busiest day as a 'thank you' for your shoppers. Personally, I would choose Fridays. Like 'Thank God it's Friday.'"

"I like that idea. We can advertise 'TGIF Cookie Day' on Fridays and see what happens."

Christie and Doris high-fived each other for their clever-ness and took another cookie. Doris selected another order to fill, and Christie straightened the card rack. It was always a bit messy after customers had rummaged through it, looking for the perfect cards.

The store phone rang. Doris exclaimed, "I'll get it. I'm closer."

A couple of minutes later, Christie walked back to see what the call had been about. She noticed her aunt's ashen face.

"It was Mr. Raspy Voice again."

THIRTY-NINE

Christie groaned. "I was hoping we were done with him. Okay, Auntie. What did he say this time? Tell me as precisely as you can remember."

"It's pretty easy. He asked for a bouquet using three specific flowers, plus whatever I want for fillers."

"Which flowers did he name?"

"Cyclamen, rudbeckia and orange lilies."

"He didn't name the colors of the first two?"

"No, honey. Just the orange lilies."

Christie felt a shiver up her spine. "He ordered orange lilies the last time. I remember they can mean revenge."

"Or pride or wealth or confidence," added Aunt Doris. "But I'm sure that's not his message."

Christie found the folder with the common meanings of flowers. "Cyclamen can mean deep love or sincerity. That's nice." She looked up and smiled. "But can also be sent to tell someone 'goodbye,' or 'it's over.' That's not so nice."

"I think of resilience and survival for rudbeckia," said her aunt. "They're a tough species. What else does your guide say?"

"Endurance and justice. Those aren't scary interpretations unless the intended message is that murdering someone is a form of justice."

"I think you should call your policeman friend, Christie."

"I will. Did Mr. Raspy Voice say when Mr. Jones would pick them up?"

"Sometime later today. And, no, he didn't give me a phone number. I didn't bother to ask."

CHIEF CONWAY LISTENED to Christie's report of another call from the mysterious flower orderer. He told her he would drive down Main Street every fifteen minutes or so starting at about four. Christie had told him that the two previous bouquets had been picked up shortly before closing time and guessed it would be the same for order number three. She promised to call his personal cell if Mr. Jones came in between Conway's rounds.

When she asked about the vehicles used by Mr. Jones in the earlier encounters, Chief Conway told her he didn't have any new information.

"That's the best we can do, I suppose," said Christie after clueing in her aunt. "You can take the picture when he comes in. Surreptitiously, of course."

Doris harrumphed. "I'm not sure I can work the newfangled security camera Anita installed, but I'll try."

Christie spent the next few minutes showing her aunt the simple procedure for taking a photo with the camera that was focused on customers when they were making their purchases. She wished she had a long trigger switch hidden under the counter as she'd had with her first camera, an old Minolta SLR 101, which she'd inherited from her dad. It reminded her that professional photographers sometimes used such a device.

"Okay. I think I can do it," said her aunt. "But maybe it would be smarter if I handle the counter and *you* operate the camera."

"That's not a bad idea, Auntie. We'll play it by ear."

THE CLOCK SEEMED to move more slowly than usual, although Christie knew it was only because of the anticipation of seeing Mr. Jones again. Shortly after four, she saw a police patrol car cruising down the street. Although it had seemed like a good idea at the time, she began to worry that the presence of the patrol car might throw a wrench into the plans to catch Mr. Jones in the act. A few minutes later, Jason pulled up in front of the shop. He was grinning broadly as he entered and approached Christie at the counter.

"Hi, Jason. You're smiling like you know something."

"I do, indeed. Do you want to guess?"

"You've found Missy!"

"No, not exactly."

"You've found an address or phone for her."

"No, not that either."

"I give. What do you know?"

"Remember you asked me to track down her brothers?"

"Of course. Have you located them?"

"Les, the investigator, was able to find the youngest of the three. The other two were quite a bit older and have already passed. But one brother, Timothy, is alive and well and lives in Moses Lake." Jason handed Christie an index card.

She read it quickly. "Has anyone talked with him?"

"Not yet. That's *your* assignment."

"Hmm. Moses Lake is about four hours from here if I drive, and I'd have to ask Aunt Doris to manage the store all day. That's too much to ask of her. I'll give him a call instead." Christie stepped out from behind the counter and threw her arms around Jason's neck. "Thank you! Thank you!"

Jason blushed.

Aunt Doris emerged from her flower room. "What's going on?"

Christie shared the news. "Maybe I'll finally be able to connect Missy and Brian after all."

"If the brother knows how to reach her and is willing to let you talk with her," admonished her aunt.

"I certainly hope so. I'll keep my fingers crossed."

Jason turned to leave. "Would you like to join me for drinks after work today?"

Christie relaxed her shoulders and smiled. "Sure. Is seven okay?"

"I'll pick you up."

THE PATROL CAR cruised through the short downtown Main Street a second time. Conway waved at Jason, who was getting into his car.

Five minutes later, a black Jeep parked across the street. A man wearing a navy parka and a knit hat jumped out, looked both ways and walked toward the flower shop. Christie held her breath, certain she was going to give herself away if this was the man who was to pick up the flowers. He approached the entrance, paused and looked both ways again, then entered. He walked directly to the sales counter. It was the same man who had picked up the two earlier orders.

"Hello. Can I help you with anything?" Christie forced herself to talk in a normal tone. He might be someone simply picking up flowers for his wife, after all.

"Do you have an order for Mr. Jones?" His voice was deep but not raspy.

"Yes, I do. Just a moment, and I'll get them for you." Christie walked quickly to the cooler and whispered to her aunt. "You can do the transaction. I'll take the picture. Stall a couple of minutes so I can call Conway."

Aunt Doris walked over to the flower cooler and made a show of selecting first one vase, then a second, and finally a third one before pronouncing, "Here it is!" She adjusted the ribbon bow and said to Christie loudly, "I'll take care of ringing it up for you so you can take care of that other order."

She walked stiffly to the counter with her arthritic joints and said cheerfully, "That'll be sixty-two dollars and twenty-three cents. Will it be cash or a credit card today?"

Mr. Jones pulled out his well-worn wallet and shuffled through the bills. He handed Doris three twenties and a five, said, "Keep the change," and picked up the vase.

"Oh, please let me put that in a box for you so it doesn't spill," said Doris. "It'll only take a moment." She grabbed a square floral delivery box from under the counter and set about stuffing paper around the vase to keep it stable. "There you go, sir. Now it'll travel better."

He mumbled, "Thanks," and carried the box under his arm.

Christie joined Doris at the counter in time to see Conway's car slowly drive past the shop and pull into a parking space. Mr. Jones backed out of his parking spot and headed west toward the freeway. Conway did a U-turn and followed shortly thereafter. Christie saw that he was talking on his radio as he drove by.

FORTY

Christie and Jason entered the Mill City Grill, which was notably quiet, even for a Monday. "Where is everybody?" Christie asked the barmaid.

She shrugged. "Beats me. But it's halfway between paychecks for a lot of the mill workers, so they may have run out of beer money by now. What are you having?"

Christie ordered a house cabernet while Jason opted for a seasonal Samuel Adams beer, Oktoberfest it was called.

"Have you called Timothy Stewart yet?" Jason asked after clinking her glass.

Christie shook her head before taking a sip of her wine. "I wanted to be sure he had enough time to get home and have dinner before I called."

"There's no time like the present if you want to call now. I won't mind."

"You're right. I'll do it." She took a big sip of her cabernet and pulled her cell and the index card from her handbag. She glanced at Jason. "Wish me luck."

She punched in the number. Two rings later, she heard, "This is Father Timothy."

Christie's eyes widened. She recovered quickly and said, "Father Timothy, this is Christie O'Mara from White Castle. I own the flower shop there. You don't know me, but I hope you can tell me how to get in touch with your sister, Missy."

Silence on the other end. After what seemed a long time, he said, "Tell me how you know Missy."

Christie told him about finding the note, about meeting Brian, and how Missy's mother had hung up on her. "I don't want to intrude into her life, but I'd like to solve the mystery of this desk and the note."

Father Timothy said quietly, "She and I chat regularly. I have a feeling she'll want to hear what you have to say. I'll have her call you. Goodbye now."

Christie put her phone down on the table and sat quietly for a moment, taking it all in.

"Are you okay?" she heard Jason ask.

She didn't trust herself to talk for a moment, so she nodded her head briskly, then said, "You didn't tell me her brother is a priest. He's going to have Missy call me. What will I say to her?"

"The same thing you said to her brother. It worked on him, didn't it? And I didn't know he was a priest."

BOTH OF THEM were quiet during the short drive back to Christie's house.

Jason lingered at Christie's door, seemingly reluctant to leave. Christie didn't want to end the day abruptly after all he'd done to help her, so she invited him in for cookies and hot chocolate. Stormy sniffed at his feet for a couple of minutes, then jumped on the sofa next to him. She arched her back and purred, demanding his attention.

By the time Christie appeared with a tray of cookies and two mugs, Stormy had made herself comfortable. She was snuggled up and purring loudly on his lap. "I see that Stormy has decided you're okay. She doesn't purr for just anybody."

Jason chuckled. "I'm glad she has black fur. It won't show as much on my dark pants."

Christie put two cookies each on napkins that pronounced "Go big or go home" and sat in the armchair on the other side of the coffee table. "It's funny that even though we were classmates all through junior high and high school, we really don't know each other well at all."

"Well, I was pretty shy and wasn't into sports. I didn't think girls liked me very much. You seemed to be popular, being a cheerleader and all that. I would never have asked you out. I was afraid you'd say no." Jason bit into a cookie. "Yum. This is great!"

"Thanks. One of my few talents." She continued, "I wasn't a great student like you were, and being a good cheerleader was like a substitute for good grades. The boys who asked me out usually thought I was some 'hot body' and didn't understand that I had a brain as well. I was motivated to go to college and get a degree so I could support myself. Most of the time, they didn't ask again, or I said 'No' when they did."

Jason nodded. "So, back to cheerleaders. Many girls in high school don't get past that stage of growing up."

"You could probably say the same thing for most of the jocks of our day. But you and I seemed to have turned out all right after all." Christie raised her mug to Jason's. "Cheers."

They grinned at each other and took swigs of the smooth cocoa.

"I was surprised when my mom told me you had reopened

the flower shop. I figured that once you made the big move to the big city, you were never coming back."

Christie raised a shoulder. "San Francisco wasn't the wonderful experience I thought it would be. It was expensive and big, and I discovered that the men there were no different from those high school jocks. When my grandmother died, I had already been thinking about making a change. The flower shop was my happy place when I was growing up, and it is again now that it's mine."

"I've already told you why I came back. Seattle wasn't for me either."

Christie's phone buzzed in her pocket. She frowned at the screen. "I don't know this number. But it says 'Washington State-verified.'"

"It could be Missy."

Christie bit her lip, swallowed hard and said, "Hello. This is Christie."

FORTY-ONE

"Hello? Is this Christie from the flower shop?"

"Yes, it is. Can I help you?"

"This is Teresa Stewart. My brother Timothy said you'd called and that I should talk with you. Is this a good time?"

Christie sat back in the chair. "Hi, Teresa. Yes, this is a perfect time."

"My brother said you called me 'Missy.' No one except him has called me that in a long time."

"Is it okay if I call you that? Or do you prefer Teresa?"

"Please call me Missy. Timothy said you have some news for me."

Over the next fifteen minutes, Christie told Missy about the desk and the note and Bronco Carver and Brian Stone and JoJo's Coffee Shop. She told her about finding out her real name from the English teacher, Mrs. Fremmerlid, and calling her parents, who had hung up on her.

"Sandra, the waitress," Christie continued, "said Brian had

given the note to her, thinking she could give it to if you went to JoJo's."

"No, I left town in such a hurry that it didn't occur to me that he would have left anything with her. But I didn't leave him a note either. Brian left in a hurry also. I thought he figured out I was pregnant and wasn't willing to be responsible for the baby."

"He said he didn't know about that until I told him. The reason he left town was because of a fight at the bar where he and a buddy had gone to have drinks after work, and some guy started yelling at him and using a cue stick as a weapon. The sheriff came, and everyone scattered except Bronco, the one guy who was still holding a cue stick. He got arrested."

"Do you know what the fight was about?" asked Missy. "It had to be something serious for Brian to just leave."

"I understand it was about you."

"Me? Why me?"

"I guess the other guy thought you should be *his* girl."

"Really? Who was it? I didn't date anyone else."

"I don't know yet. I'm still working on that part."

"Timothy said you've talked with Brian. Where is he?"

"He's in Easton. I have a phone number if you want to call him. Where are *you* living, if you don't mind my asking?"

"I ended up in Olympia. It was too painful to stay in Spokane, knowing I might run into my daughter someday. Having two sons later when I got married helped ease the loss, but they're all grown up and out of the house. I've been alone since their father died of cancer a few years ago."

"I'm sorry about your losses. Do you want Brian's number?"

Missy promised to come to White Castle to visit in the near future. By the end of the conversation, Christie felt like they had been friends for a long time.

Christie shared the information with Jason, who was just as eager as she was to meet the woman who had only been a name until twenty minutes ago.

"Her brother's a priest, which means she was probably raised Catholic. Being single and pregnant would have been a major blow to her parents. I'm guessing they encouraged her to have the baby in another town since abortion would have been taboo, and they didn't want to lose face. That may have made it difficult for Missy to have a loving relationship with her parents after giving the baby up for adoption."

"But does she have a good relationship with them now?"

"I didn't get that impression when I talked with her. You know, I just had another thought."

"And that is?"

"What if one of both of Missy's brothers were involved in the bar fight? You know, defending the honor of a sister. They would have been strangers to the bartender."

"Maybe, but I would hate to think one of them could have been a murderer," said Jason quietly.

"You're right. Erase that thought."

"Well, Christie. You can talk with Missy about her family someday, but right now, I'm going to leave," said Jason. "I'm sure you want to call Anita and your mom and whoever else is on your need-to-know list."

"Thank you, Jason. That's thoughtful of you. I *would* like some time to just sit and think. I can't believe we've actually found both Missy and Brian." Christie sighed and flopped back in the chair. A moment later, she sat up straight. "But we still need to find the real murderer. Our job isn't done yet."

"Is it really necessary?" Jason stood up, scooting Stormy off his lap as he did so.

"Yes." Christie arose to face him. "Bronco told us he wasn't guilty, and I believe him. Brian helped confirm that."

"Okay. I get it. What else do you need Les to find out?"

"Do you think he could talk to some of those other men who were at the bar that night? I know a couple of them are no longer alive, but there's got to be someone who can give us a lead."

Jason exhaled loudly. "And you're not going to be satisfied until Bronco has been absolved, are you?"

Christie smiled, hands on her hips. "You may just know me well enough, after all."

CHRISTIE WRESTLED with calling Anita versus her mother next. She flipped a mental coin and called her friend. Anita was busy correcting papers for her English AP literature class.

"Do you realize how many of these intelligent students can't spell 'Shakespeare' correctly?" Anita wailed. "I hate to dock them for misspelled words, but I have to. They won't get any leniency from their college professors, so it's up to me to prepare them for the cruel world."

"Good for you. Speaking of the cruel world, I heard from Missy tonight."

"Missy? *The* Missy? Tell me more!"

Christie shared what she'd learned, ending with, "She lives in Olympia. That's where Jason said her daughter is living."

"Oh my gosh! Do you suppose they know each other and don't realize the relationship?"

"I don't know yet. And I didn't think to tell Missy that detail. Brian knows, however, and I gave her his phone number so she'll find out from him. Maybe that's better anyway."

"Well, it sounds like there's a happy ending to your little mystery after all. Good work, Christie."

"Thanks, except you're forgetting there's still someone out there who killed Arnold Youngman, the guy in the bar. Because I'm convinced Bronco didn't do it."

FORTY-TWO

Tuesday morning began with a bang, or more precisely, a rumble of thunder that rolled through the clouds. Jagged streaks of lightning pierced the sky every few minutes, followed by more thunder. Christie counted the seconds between the sight and the sounds: six seconds. The storm was six miles away, according to her calculations. She anticipated a slow day at the shop with weather that would almost surely be wet and nasty. True thunderstorms were rare in her part of the country. And they were exciting in a way, with Mother Nature having her way with the world.

Aunt Doris was already at work, busy creating tabletop decorations for a women's luncheon at the Methodist Church. She tucked shortened stems of gold and burgundy chrysanthemums into squat, square glass vases that already sported mauve carnations. A few pieces of greenery and a couple of twigs completed the simple but beautiful arrangement.

"Those are lovely, Auntie. You have a marvelous talent for making gorgeous designs out of simple elements." Christie picked up several flowers, shortened the stems, and laid them on the counter, ready for her aunt.

Her aunt looked up and smiled as she said, "It just comes naturally. I was lucky that your grandmother had a flower shop so I could do what I love every day. She took me in when I didn't have any place to go after both of my parents died in a car crash. I was still in high school. Most young women didn't go to college in those days. Maude had already married my older brother, your grandpa, so they let me stay with them and be a nanny to her children and help with the cooking and all."

"How did she decide to start the flower shop?" Christie asked while cutting more stems. "It seems like it's always been here."

"Once your mother and her brothers were on their own, she was bored. She'd always had a sense for business, so she scouted out a location, dreamed up a plan and convinced your grandpa that she could run a flower business. He had a little money set aside that he let her 'borrow' as though it were a loan and gave her one year to pay it back."

"Let me guess. She paid it back in six months."

"Nope. It only took her three months. Your grandpa was surprised, and after that, he talked like the business was his idea in the first place." Aunt Doris chuckled. "But we all knew better. I've always had a hunch she wanted to give me something to do, too, so I could feel more independent since I never married or had children of my own." She dried her hands and put an arm around Christie's shoulders. "That's what families do, you know."

Christie felt the warmth of her aunt's hug. "And now you're helping me."

"Now, you let me finish these so they'll be ready when Marianne comes to get them." Aunt Doris swooshed Christie out of her flower room.

The front door chime rang. Christie looked up to see Chief Conway enter.

She walked toward him. "Were you able to follow the guy with the flowers yesterday?"

"Yeah. It turns out he didn't go very far. He drove to the nursing home on Adams Street. He was in and out pretty fast. When I went inside and asked about them, the head nurse said she was told they were for one of the residents."

"Did you ask about the resident? Were you able to get a name?"

"I couldn't exactly ask for the name because of those HIPAA laws, and I didn't have cause legally otherwise."

Christie rolled her eyes. "Well, thanks anyway. I'm sorry to have caused you any trouble."

"It's okay. The way I see it, there have been two deaths that seem to be related to your flowers, but maybe it's just a coincidence. On the other hand, I understand how this could hurt your business if people stop ordering your flowers."

"Thank you for that. I hope it stops." Christie sighed. "Do you want me to call if I get another order from Mr. Raspy Voice?"

"Sure. I'm curious as well, but I think you're making a bigger deal out of the messages than they deserve." Conway saluted with two fingers on the brim of his hat, smiled, and left.

Christie was disappointed that Conway had met a barrier. She considered the possibility that one of those nursing home residents had been at the bar that night and might have been a witness. Was someone killing them off? And if so, why now, after all these years? Would there be yet another victim? Helpless to do anything about it, she went to work putting in an order for flower stock. She was still fuming under the surface, but she knew she couldn't call the home herself. She decided that she would follow the man herself if she had another order from Mr. Raspy Voice. And call Conway, just in case.

"I know you're disappointed, Christie," said Aunt Doris, "but I suppose he's right about what he said. Maybe we're overthinking those messages."

"Or maybe there'll be another death." Christie stabbed the order button. "I might have to follow the next delivery myself."

"Ooh. I don't think that's a very good idea. You leave that up to Chief Conway."

Christie calmed down over the next hour as a steady stream of customers came in. Some were probably only coming in to get out of the heavy rain, but most of them purchased at least a card. She reminded herself that small purchases multiplied many times over were just as valuable as the occasional large purchase.

It was almost time to close up shop when Brian Stone called her personal cell number.

"Hello. This is Christie."

"This is Brian Stone."

Christie almost dropped the phone. "Hi! It's nice to hear from you. What's up?"

"Hey. I'm just calling to thank you and let you know that Missy called me last night. We had a long conversation, and we're going to meet for lunch on Friday. She sounds just the same as she did all those years ago. I can't believe you found her."

Christie squealed. "I just love happy endings! I'll want to hear about it later. So, did you ever call Lynette? I didn't tell Missy that I thought we'd found her daughter. I didn't want to disappoint her if she wasn't the right person."

"I tried her office number, but so far, we haven't connected. Her secretary said she was out of the office for meetings but wouldn't tell me when she would be back."

"If you're meeting Missy in Olympia, maybe you could drop in at Lynette's office. Those 'meetings' could be a standard reply to unknown callers like you or me."

Brian laughed. "I've used a similar excuse myself, except I was always 'in the library.'"

"I hope you have a wonderful visit."

Christie ended the call and floated to the flower room, where Aunt Doris was tidying up the bits and pieces of the last project of the day.

Her aunt looked up as Christie approached her table. "You're grinning like you just won a million dollars, honey. What's happened?"

"Auntie, you're not going to believe this."

FORTY-THREE

After taking care of Stormy's dinner, Christie treated herself to a glass of wine while preparing her own meal of sautéed chicken, steamed broccoli and fresh French bread she'd picked up on her way home. After enjoying the simple meal, she was eager to talk about her call from Brian but hadn't decided whether to tell Anita or Jason first. When her cell phone rang, the decision was made for her; Jason was on the line.

"Hi, Christie. Did you hear from Brian today?"

"Yes, this afternoon. Did he call you too?"

"That he did. He was pretty excited that he was going to be meeting Missy after all these years."

"Knowing that they're getting together again makes my heart feel warm and fuzzy."

"It might not work out for them, you know. There's been a lot of time that might have changed things."

"True," said Christie, "but I choose to believe that love will prevail. When I asked, Brian said he hadn't been able to talk to Lynette yet."

"Have you told Missy about possibly finding her daughter yet?"

"I thought it might be better for Brian to talk to her about that, so I didn't say anything. I would hate to cause unnecessary disappointment for her."

"You're probably right. Well, I have a meeting with a client, so gotta run. I'd love to have dinner with you this weekend if that's okay with you."

"I'd love it, Jason. Bye."

A FEW MINUTES LATER, her personal phone rang again. She considered ignoring it — she was bombarded with spam calls — until she saw Chief Conway's name and thought maybe he was calling to give her some new information. She answered. "Hi, Conway. What's up?"

"Remember when you asked me about tracing calls to your shop, and I told you it was a cumbersome process?"

"Of course I do. I presume you've discovered something to tell me."

"Through a process of elimination and cross-references, my IT man determined that there have been three calls made from the public library to your business on the three days you reported getting the calls."

"I'm pretty sure no one from the library has ordered any flowers. Did you ask the head librarian?"

"I did, and she assured me that the calls weren't made by any of her staff."

"And I presume that it's going to be difficult to pinpoint who made those calls. Right?"

"Correct, except that the extension that was used is only

available to the staff and the volunteers, not the general public."

"Has she come up with the name yet?"

"Not yet, but she is checking the volunteer schedule against the days the flowers were ordered to see if she can identify the most likely candidate."

"That's progress! Thank you for letting me know."

CHRISTIE TIDIED up her kitchen before making a call to Anita. She was feeling at loose ends and wanted to share the latest news with her, especially with Conway's revelation about the calls coming from the library. But would it be another dead end?

Anita was grading another set of papers, this time for the junior English class. "When I was in high school, I didn't appreciate how much time our teachers spent out of class time preparing lessons, grading papers, talking to parents and counseling students. I'm ready to support pay raises!"

"And it's only November!"

"Yes, and elections are around the corner. I'm going to be scrutinizing everyone's comments closely to see whether or not they support paying more for education. But I'm sure that's not why you called. What's on your mind?"

Christie summarized her conversations with Jason and Conway.

"The calls came from the library? That doesn't make any sense."

"It does if the caller wanted to remain anonymous."

"But then what? Were those calls illegal?"

"No, but they might be if they end up being related to a couple of deaths. Which has yet to be proven, of course."

"I can see the headline now: KILLER FLOWERS STRIKE LOCAL RESIDENTS," said Anita with a giggle.

"Anita, it's not funny. At least, not to me or about my business."

"I'm teasing. I think my brain is getting mushy from reading these essays. I now know why college professors hire teachers' assistants to help them do the grading."

CHRISTIE AND STORMY resumed their normal positions in the living room — human in the chair with feline curled up on her lap — while watching a *Blue Bloods* episode. The storyline was about seemingly unrelated people dying. When the detectives dug deeper, they discovered that the victims had all served on the same jury twenty years before. Christie shivered. Was it possible that a similar plot was being played out in White Castle? But by whom? And why now?

 CHAPTER

FORTY-FOUR

Jason called Christie at the shop early Wednesday.

"I have to be in court most of the day, but I wanted to let you know that Les was able to track down a few more of the witnesses from forty years ago. Three others that he identified have already died, including Jerry Ferguson. Do you want their names?"

"Of course I do!"

Jason rattled off a half dozen names. "He hasn't talked with all of them, but he plans to do so as soon as he locates them."

"People just don't stay in one place anymore," said Christie. "I was watching a *Blue Bloods* rerun last night, and it made me think about another motive for the flowers. What if Mr. Raspy Voice is targeting jury members from 1982?"

"That's an interesting premise, but that would mean Bronco Carver was the killer, and you and I both believe he is truly innocent."

"Innocent of the murder of Youngman back then," said Christie, "but could he be getting revenge now? On the jury that convicted him wrongly?"

"It's possible, I suppose. I'll see if I can track down the jurors' names, but it might require getting a subpoena. Don't hold your breath on this one. And if it were the jurors, why would Jerry Ferguson be a target? He would have been a witness, not in the jury box."

"But wasn't he one of the men who ran off? So, he never did testify to help exonerate Bronco. But I suppose you're right. Like I said, it was just a thought."

"I'll still see what I can find."

"Thanks, Jason. And thanks for the names you gave me. I'm not sure how it helps, but it fills in a few more puzzle pieces anyway. I hope your day goes well."

"Me too. I've got a custody battle today, and I'm worried it might get ugly."

"And the kids get caught in the middle."

"True. I'll let you know when I hear from Les again."

A SIREN PIERCED THE AIR. A moment later, the ambulance's red and white lights flashed as it raced up the street in front of Christie's shop.

"I wonder who needs help," said Aunt Doris from the flower room.

"It's not going toward the freeway," replied Christie, "so it's probably a local resident. I hope it's nothing serious."

Aunt Doris answered the shop's phone as Christie updated the order sheet for items that her aunt had listed on the replacement list. She needed both small and medium-sized vases, various colors of wide ribbon, and green florist's foam. Christie was grateful for fast delivery from the wholesale house in Portland. In earlier days, Maude had driven to the warehouse every Sunday. Christie recalled how her grandmother made a special day of it, sometimes stopping at the Jantzen Beach Mall with its merry-go-round and getting ice cream cones. She'd always order mint chocolate chip, and Grandma Maude ordered strawberry. Just plain strawberry. She found herself smiling at the memory.

She winced when she heard her aunt slam the phone receiver into the cradle. "It's him," she said with an edge to her voice.

"*Who* 'him?'"

"Mr. Raspy Voice. That's who."

Christie groaned. "What did he order this time? More orange lilies?"

"That's not funny, Christie."

"I'm sorry. It just came out of my mouth. What did he order?"

"Two bouquets of blue and yellow flowers."

"No special messages this time?"

"No. Unless you call a black ribbon a message."

"Blue and yellow makes me think of school colors, like Kelso or Cub Scouts. Or is it Boy Scouts?"

Aunt Doris snorted. "This guy ain't no Boy Scout."

"I'm going to follow whoever picks them up this time," Christie said firmly. "Will you cover the shop for me and close up if I'm not back in time?"

"Shouldn't you call Chief Conway instead?"

"This doesn't sound as ominous, but I'm still curious enough to follow him myself. And see where he goes."

"I think you had the right idea, even if it ended up wrong. By the way, what did Jason say earlier? I heard you say something about names."

"He said his private investigator had a few more names of possible witnesses at the bar fight," said Christie. "He was still working on calling those who were still alive."

"Did you recognize any of the names? Were Brian or Bronco on the list?"

"No. But they might mean something to you." Christie handed Doris the names she'd written down.

Doris read it quickly and shook her head. "Three of these were older men at that time. I'm sure they're all dead by now. I don't recognize the other names."

Christie sighed. "Another dead end."

The front door chimed, and Conway hurried in.

"Good morning, Chief," said Christie cheerfully before noticing the dark look in his eyes. "What is it?"

"I just came from the nursing home where your flowers were delivered on Monday. One of the residents took a turn for the worse and was sent to the hospital this morning. The nurse recalled how I had been wanting to know that resident's name because he had been the one who got the bouquet. So she thought to call me with this outcome. She said he was having chest pains and could barely talk."

"No!" Christie cried as Doris came forward from the flower room. "Do you have a name?"

Conway pulled his notebook from his shirt pocket. "Kevin Tyler. Do you know him?"

Christie gasped and covered her mouth. "He's on the list of witnesses that Jason gave me earlier this morning."

"Witnesses to what?"

"The cue stick murder in 1982." Christie showed him the short list.

Conway read the names, nodding grimly.

"Jerry Ferguson was also a witness," said Christie, "and he's dead."

Aunt Doris said, "I know our flowers can't hurt people, so what's going on?"

Christie searched her brain for possible explanations. "Could he have had a visitor, or was there a medication error?"

"I'll have the detective investigate," said Conway, "but for now, I don't think it was the flowers. At least not directly. Goodbye now."

Conway was out the door and backing out of the parking space before Christie thought of the new order they'd gotten. There was no specific message requested this time, or was there? Black ribbons might mean death. But whose death?

FORTY-FIVE

Mr. Jones parked in front of the shop shortly after four thirty. He looked both ways down the street before crossing the sidewalk and entering. He paused just inside the door and appeared to take note of any other shoppers. Christie felt her heart speed up. It was the same man who picked up the last bouquet. She waited until he asked for the bouquets, then went to the cooler to retrieve them and whispered to her aunt, "It's the same guy as last time. I'll leave as soon as you go up to the desk. I'll have my cell with me if you need to call."

"Here are you, sir," Aunt Doris said as Christie collected her handbag from the back room. "That'll be one hundred twenty-five dollars and six cents including tax. Cash or charge?"

Christie slipped quietly out the back door and jumped into her car. She sped up the alley and waited at the end, ready to follow. Mr. Jones was backing out of his spot, presumably unaware that she was watching him. He turned right at the end of the street and headed toward the freeway on-ramp, with Christie one car behind him. *Where is he going?* She merged into traffic and kept an eye on his SUV as he drove. He maintained a speed of seventy-two miles per hour, a smidge over the speed limit.

About twenty miles farther north, he took the off-ramp where a gas station, café and a vacant fireworks stand held court. The SUV pulled into the lot in front of the fireworks stand and stopped. Christie waited in front of the café and watched. A few minutes passed by. Several vehicles exited the freeway and went to either the gas station or the café. Another few minutes later, a black pickup, a late-model Ford F-150, pulled up next to the SUV, driver's door to driver's door. Christie watched as the blue and yellow bouquets were passed from the SUV to the truck. She also saw a small manila envelope pass from the SUV to the pickup.

The SUV drove off, but not before Christie wrote down the license plate number. The pickup waited a couple of minutes, then drove off, going north on the freeway. Christie wrote down the second number.

She followed the pickup, staying two or three vehicles behind to lessen the chance of being detected. Ten miles farther up the freeway, the pickup exited to take one of the state highways that crisscrossed the state. Christie worried that she would be noticed because of light traffic, but there was nothing she could do but stay back far enough to be less noticeable but close enough that she could see if her prey took a side road.

She was driving through farm country. Small farms with barns, herds of cattle, a few horses, and the occasional pond spotted the landscape as she maintained a safe distance. Her phone rang.

"This is Christie," she said, grateful her car was equipped with Bluetooth.

"Oh, I'm so glad I called the right number. This is Sandra. Brian's friend?"

"Yes, Sandra. What's on your mind?"

"I finally remembered who I gave Brian's note to. My memory was a little fuzzy, and I kept trying to see his face, but I couldn't pinpoint it until today."

"Who was it?"

"Jack Smith. The deputy sheriff's son. He said he knew Missy and promised to give it to her."

Christie felt her heart skip. "Thanks, Sandra. I'll take care of it from here. You stay safe."

Christie debated calling Conway, which would require her to stop for a moment and pull up his contact info, versus continuing her pursuit. She didn't know who she was following but had memorized the plate and would report it to Conway as soon as she was able. And tell him about Jack Smith. She didn't want to lose sight of the black pickup, so she kept driving through the tall firs and cedars on both sides of the two-lane highway.

AUNT DORIS GLANCED at the clock for the fourth time in the last hour. She hadn't heard a word from Christie and was a bit concerned. Her headstrong great-niece wasn't always good about letting others know what she was up to. Conway called just before five.

"May I speak to Christie, please?"

"She's not here. Can I take a message?"

"Doris, I really need to talk with her directly. Is she on her cell?"

"Yes, sir. She's following the guy who picks up flowers for Mr. Raspy Voice."

"She's *what?*"

"She didn't want to bother you again after the goose chase a couple of days ago, so she decided to follow him herself."

"Do you have any idea where she went?"

"No, but she followed the same SUV you tailed that went to the nursing home. I recognized it and the man. So you should have that plate number."

"I have it. I'll put an APB out for it, then I'll call her on her cell. If you hear from her first, please tell her to call me. I think I know who the mysterious caller is."

Conway submitted the alert before trying Christie's number. She didn't pick up. He fumed for a moment. Then walked to the dispatcher's desk to ask for her phone to be pinged. He cooled his heels while waiting for some clue as to where she might be. From White Castle, she could have driven north or south on the freeway or east or west into the country. Or she could have started on the freeway and taken any number of side roads from there. Basically, she could be anywhere in the 360 degrees from where he stood.

CHRISTIE STAYED AS FAR BACK as she could while keeping the black pickup in sight. At one point, the truck pulled to the side of the road and sat there for a couple of minutes. Christie wondered if he was checking a map or GPS. She wasn't familiar with the area herself, except for recognizing it as one of the backroads that would eventually lead to Mount Rainier. She stopped near a driveway, and while she waited for the truck to move, she checked her phone for messages. To her dismay, she discovered she was in one of those dead zones in the rural part of the state. Being surrounded by trees didn't help matters any.

The pickup finally moved, and so did Christie. In a few

minutes, she was driving along pastures again, and then a popular wholesale nursery. Her phone rang, startling her.

"Hello. This is Christie."

"Conway here. Where are you?"

"Somewhere east of the freeway on Highway 12. I'm following a black pickup." She told him about the flower transfer and recited the pickup's plate number.

"I got a message from the librarian. She thinks the person who called the orders in is one of the volunteers."

"Who was it?" Christie asked into the phone as she entered another dead zone.

FORTY-SIX

Conway called one of his friends at the State Patrol office and alerted him to the situation. The trooper promised to notify the sheriff of the county where Christie's car had been pinpointed. He had run the plates through the state system and knew who she was following, assuming the driver was the registered owner. He left the station with lights flashing and siren blaring.

CHRISTIE MAINTAINED a separation from the black pickup she was following. She wondered where he was heading, but when she saw a sign that indicated Easton was five miles ahead, she knew. He had to be delivering the flowers to Brian Stone. Or was it Bronco Carver? Or both, since there were two bouquets. But who was driving? As far as she knew, the only other person who knew Brian's location was Bronco Carver. And possibly Missy or Lynette if they had done some online searches. But was it likely that a female would be Mr. Raspy Voice?

She tried calling Conway but was in another dead zone, which was common on the country roads and highways when surrounded by tall cedars, firs and pines. She hit her fist on the steering wheel and kept her eye on the pickup. She noted a helicopter above and wondered if it was from the airbase, which was only about fifty miles away by air. Or a Forest Service chopper monitoring illegal hunting or logging.

Before long, she saw lights flashing and heard sirens behind her. She glanced at her speedometer and wondered if the patrol car was pursuing her, but she was barely five miles per hour over the speed limit of sixty on this stretch of highway. She shrugged and kept driving. Another couple of minutes later, the patrol car pulled alongside and signaled to her to pull over. Confused, she complied and waited in her car, fuming, until the officer came to the driver's side window. She was frustrated that she had lost sight of the Ford F-150, which had continued down the road.

Instead of asking for her driver's license and registration as was usual for a traffic stop, the State Patrolman asked if she was Christie O'Mara. Surprised that he knew her name, she responded affirmatively.

"What is it, Officer?"

"I need you to follow me, Miss O'Mara."

"Why?"

"Just follow me, please." He walked back to his car and pulled in front of her, signaling for her to follow.

Christie reluctantly did as requested and stayed as close behind as she felt comfortable, considering that the patrol car had lights and sirens on and he was driving at a brisk eighty miles per hour. Shortly before entering the city limits of Easton, he slowed down and signaled a right turn. Christie followed suit. A few blocks later, he pulled into a parking lot where a county sheriff's car sat with the engine idling. She stopped next to the county sheriff, popped out of her car, and ran up to the state trooper.

"What's going on?" she asked. "Why did you pull me over? I was trying to follow a truck, and now I've lost it."

"There's a situation that has developed that I'm not authorized to share at this moment."

"What situation? I'm trying to find out who's been ordering flowers that end up with people dying!" Christie stood with her feet apart and arms down, fists clenched.

"Yes, Miss. So are we."

"Huh?" She relaxed a little.

"Police Chief Conway notified our office and alerted us to the problem. He's on his way here as well."

"How are you going to help if you're here and not following the pickup?"

Christie turned her head when she heard another vehicle enter the lot. She watched Chief Conway step out of his police car, then ran over to him. "What are *you* doing here? What's going on?"

"Come with me," he said. Conway put an arm around her shoulders and walked with her to rejoin the state trooper. "I got your message, and when I discovered who owned the vehicle, I alerted one of my friends in the Olympia State Patrol office. He notified the local county sheriff and set up a pursuit."

"Who have I been following?" Christie asked again.

"Well, we don't know yet who's driving the car, but we know who the registered owner is."

"Are you going to tell me who it is?"

"I'll get to that in a moment." Conway continued, "I don't know if you saw the helicopter, but it's doing aerial surveillance for us while the ground pursuit continues."

"Bronco Carver and Brian Stone both live somewhere up here," said Christie. "One of them is probably the target recipient of the flowers. Or it could be both because there are two bouquets."

Conway nodded. "I called your friend, Jason, at his office, and he filled me in. He told me to tell you to be careful, by the way." He winked and smiled. "We have police stationed near each of their homes, ready to intervene when the pickup shows up."

"What if he goes somewhere else? What if this isn't related at all?"

"You worry too much. We have backup plans and more backup plans. Trust me. Okay, Christie?"

Christie exhaled loudly. "And you're going to make me stay here, aren't you?"

"Of course. But I'll keep you posted. Let's go inside the station and wait. It shouldn't be long now."

Christie called her aunt to apprise her of the pursuit. She tried to talk to Jason, but he was in a hearing at the courthouse. Twenty minutes passed.

Conway talked on his cell phone every few minutes but didn't share any of his conversations with her. After another ten minutes and another chat on his phone, he finally said to Christie, "The suspect is in custody. It's safe for you to go back to White Castle while I take care of some business here."

"Don't I get to know who it is?"

"Not just yet, Christie. You'll have to be patient. I'll be in touch."

FORTY-SEVEN

As soon as Christie entered the back door, Aunt Doris dropped the flower stems onto her work table, dried her hands and rushed over to give her a hug.

"Thank God you're safe! Did Chief Conway get in touch with you?" she asked. "He called here a couple of hours ago."

"Yes he did. He caught up with me on Highway 12 and told me the man I was following was finally apprehended. He couldn't give me the name yet, however. Privacy and all that."

"I was worried when I didn't hear from you at first, so I told him you were following Mr. Jones. He took it from there."

Christie picked up Stormy, who had jumped down from her perch, and nuzzled her fur. "I was surprised to be stopped by the sheriff until Conway explained what happened." She coaxed Stormy into her carrier and grabbed her aunt's coat from the hook.

"It's time for all of us to go home. Thank you, Auntie, for staying late and taking care of things."

"I figured you would have to come here first to get Stormy

before going home. And I wanted to be here when you came in."

Christie hugged her aunt with her free arm. "Thank you for worrying! I hit a few dead zones when I went through the tall timber and didn't think to check for missed calls."

"That's okay. I'm glad you're all right."

"Yes, I am. I'll open up in the morning so you can sleep in."

Aunt Doris untied her work apron and put on her coat. "And since when have you known me to sleep in? Besides, a big order came in for a funeral on Friday. I checked the flower stock, and we'll be okay."

"Thanks. See you tomorrow."

Christie took care of a few details before setting the security system, turning off the lights, and double-checking the lock as she left.

STORMY PRESSED herself against her mistress's legs, weaving in and out while Christie opened a can of cat salmon. Her usual purring was replaced by hungry meows. Cat fed, Christie called Anita and shared the news that the waitress, Sandra, had remembered to whom she had given Brian's note.

"Jack Smith? The deputy sheriff's son? Really?"

"Yes, really, which means he obviously knew what note I had found when I talked to him the first time."

"Do you think he's the one who ordered the deadly flowers as well?"

"I don't know yet, but it certainly would seem that way. I'm hoping Chief Conway will fill me in on a couple of details, like who they took into custody in Easton."

"Easton? Why Easton?"

"I skipped parts of the story, so I'll backtrack a little."

Christie took a breath and filled Anita in on her afternoon's journey.

"Quite the adventure, girlfriend. Call me tomorrow. I've got a few more essays to read tonight."

"You bet. Bye."

Christie sat in her favorite chair for another minute, then called Jason and filled him in. She was hoping Conway had given him more information than he had given her, considering that he was an attorney, almost a fellow professional.

"No, Christie. Conway didn't tell me anything I didn't already know, so I'm in the dark as much as you are. Are you sure this guy was headed to Easton?"

"It sure looked that way, but I got stopped by a state trooper before I could find out. You realize, of course, that both Brian Stone and Bronco Carver live there now. I bet one of them, or maybe both, were the targets this time."

"Sounds plausible, but you'll have to wait to hear from Conway."

"Yeah, although patience isn't always one of my virtues."

"Let me know if you hear from him. Okay?"

"Of course. Good night, Jason."

Christie sipped on her cabernet with Stormy purring in her lap. She thought back to recent conversations involving the mystery flower orderer, Brian and Missy, and the note. She now knew that Jack Smith had intercepted the note but didn't know how the note became attached to the desk. She suspected Jack had been jealous of Brian and Missy, recalling his mention of her being "a looker" and all the guys being interested in her. Maybe Jack was as well. But was he now killing people over that? It didn't make sense. She suddenly remembered that Conway had mentioned he'd talked with the head librarian, who had thought one of her volunteers may have used the phone to call her shop. Most likely, of course, is that the person Christie followed was the same one who bought the flowers and had been heading to kill once again: the man who Conway hadn't revealed to her. But wait... Conway *had* been about to tell her when she'd been in the car. She'd entered a dead zone before he could tell her who. Christie checked the time and called Conway.

"Hey, Christie," said Conway. "I can't tell you who was taken into custody yet if that's why you're calling."

"No. It's about the library volunteer who might have ordered the flowers. I didn't catch the name because I went into a dead zone."

"Let me look at my notes. Hold on a sec." A moment later, he recited a half dozen names of the volunteers who were at the library on the days in question. "Do you recognize any of them?"

"Unfortunately, no. None of those were on the witness list that Jason got from the file records or the juror's list from the courthouse. Another dead end." Christie sighed. "When will you be able to release the name of your suspect? Will you tell me before it goes out to the public?"

"As soon as it's proper, I'll let you know."

"Thanks, Conway. At least I can reassure Aunt Doris that we won't be hearing from Mr. Raspy Voice again. She'll be happy about that."

CHAPTER

FORTY-EIGHT

Thursday morning's weather was typical for November: gray clouds with intermittent rain showers. Christie made a face at the sky and said to Stormy, "This would be a good day to fly to Hawaii, wouldn't it? Or stay home all day and sit by the fire."

Stormy purred and agreed from her cushion on the hearth, then protested a little when placed in the cat carrier for the ride to the shop.

True to form, Aunt Doris had already arrived and was busy with the funeral flower orders when Christie and Stormy dragged in through the back door.

"You seem very cheerful for such a gloomy day," said Christie as she hung her raincoat on the hook. She opened the carrier. Stormy stretched and sauntered out, then jumped up to her perch.

"I'm happy that we might be done with those orders from Mr. Raspy Voice."

"Me, too." Christie sighed as she turned on the computer. "But it doesn't feel like it's over — not until Conway tells me

226

who was detained. Or, if he was arrested, how could ordering flowers be a crime? But maybe this will at least scare Mr. Raspy Voice enough to leave us alone. That alone might be worth celebrating."

"Well, honey, right now, we both need to work on these orders to have them done by this afternoon." Doris passed an order ticket to Christie. "You can start with this one."

Christie glanced at the order, then turned on the lights for the front of the shop and unlocked the front door. She was ready for business.

By midmorning, the two women had prepared a dozen of the floral bouquets, with another dozen or so left to do. Christie prepared two cups of tea and persuaded her aunt to take a short break while she checked her email. The phone had been ringing steadily with more orders — some for the funeral and others for birthdays and other events.

Christie was scrolling through a promotion for pre-Christmas orders when she heard her aunt mumble and slam the phone down.

"What is it, Auntie?"

"Mr. Raspy Voice. That's what." Her face was fixed in a scowl. "He ordered more flowers. With an orange lily again."

"I'm calling Conway," said Christie. "He needs to know."

Christie was able to get through to him on the first try. When she finished relating the latest call, she said, "I'll do that," and hung up. "Conway wants me to call him when Mr. Jones shows up and stall him long enough to give him five minutes to get here."

"That's easy. I won't put the orange lily in till the last minute. You can tell him that we had to wait for the flower delivery to come in and hadn't had a chance to finish his order."

"That'll work. Now, let's finish those funeral flowers."

Christie paused and said grimly, "Oh, Auntie. What if these are for one of the men who died after getting one of our bouquets?"

THE REST of the day moved slowly, partly because there were only a few customers in the store and partly because of the anticipation of their mysterious Mr. Jones's impending arrival. The church bells down the street had just chimed four thirty when he entered the shop. He looked around before walking to the counter and asking for the order for Mr. Jones. He seemed a little shorter than the earlier "Mr. Jones" but was dressed similarly, albeit differently: dark trench coat, black pants, and a black fedora over his graying brown hair. His dark brown eyes darted right and left as though looking for a camera.

Christie said cheerfully, "We'll have that ready for you in just a minute. We had to wait for a delivery from the wholesaler before we could finish. I don't usually keep orange lilies in stock. Excuse me while I tell my aunt that you're here."

Christie turned and said to Doris, "Mr. Jones is here. Go ahead and add the lilies that just came in while I call the bookstore about that book I ordered." She walked to the back of the shop, pulled her phone from her pocket, and dialed Conway. "This is Ms. O'Mara. Can you tell me if the book on flowers I ordered earlier is in yet?...It's here? Great! I'll pick it up in a few minutes."

Doris fiddled with the bouquet for another couple of minutes. Mr. Jones twitched every time he heard a sound. Stormy jumped down from her shelf where she'd been napping and walked over to Mr. Jones. She arched her back, hair on end, tail flicking, and growled. Christie quickly picked up the kitty and held her in one arm while ringing up the sale with the other hand. It was a full five minutes before Doris strolled up with the flowers, and Mr. Jones had paid. He left the change on the counter and exited, walking swiftly out the door.

"Do you think we gave Conway enough time?" her aunt asked.

Christie spotted the police car approaching from the left and said, "He's halfway down the block in an unmarked car."

"Good," her aunt replied.

Christie watched Conway as he drove past the shop and then saw a red Porsche pull into the parking spot vacated by Mr. Jones. Her mouth dropped open when she saw Lynette Nichols emerge from the driver's side. "Well, look who's here." A few seconds later, the passenger door opened, and a second woman stepped out. "That's got to be Missy."

Christie hurried to the front door and held it open for the two women. "Lynette! And is this Missy? Please come in!"

After hugs all around, Christie introduced Aunt Doris, and Lynette introduced Missy.

"I'm thrilled to see you two together," said Christie. "Come on back so we can visit a few minutes before I close up for the day."

Lynette spotted the writing desk right away as she walked through the shop. She touched it lovingly. "It's still here. I thought you might have sold it."

Christie shook her head. "No. When you didn't come back, I decided to keep it as a display piece instead."

"Is it still for sale?"

Christie smiled, a glint in her eye. "I'll tell you a story about the desk if you ladies will join me at JoJo's right after we close. Aunt Doris, do you want to join us?"

Doris shook her head. "This doesn't involve me, so you go on ahead. I'll close up shop and take Stormy to your house."

Missy said, "I know right where JoJo's is. Lynette and I will see you there."

~

Chief Conway followed the black SUV through the city streets to a residential area of older homes. Having grown up in the town, he knew the owners of many of the homes that he passed as he surreptitiously drove through, letting the SUV stay at least a half block ahead of him. He talked over his radio periodically, keeping his fellow officer, Sean McLean, apprised of his location. When the SUV stopped in the middle of the block ahead, Conway turned at the corner and parked his rig out of sight. He spotted McLean's unmarked car approaching from the opposite direction and instructed him to park a few houses down across the street from the SUV's location.

Conway and McLean approached the house quickly, guns at the ready, as soon as Mr. Jones had knocked on the door and stepped inside.

FORTY-NINE

Christie, Missy and Lynette gathered at JoJo's and ordered coffee all around.

"It hasn't changed much in forty years," said Missy. "These booths are the same as when Brian and I met here in the old days." She dabbed at a wet eye and placed an arm around her daughter.

Christie sat forward, elbows on the table. "How did you two finally connect? I'm dying to know the rest of the story, as Paul Harvey used to say."

Missy and Lynette looked at each other. The resemblance was unmistakable: same nose, blue eyes, tousled auburn hair, and dimples. Missy said, "Brian called Lynette at work and left a message because she was at a meeting."

"I thought it might be a prank when I first listened to it," said Lynette, "but what he said made sense. I waited a day before calling him back and checked him out on the internet in the meantime."

"And I had talked with my brother, Father Timothy, before

calling Brian," said Missy. "He encouraged me to talk with him. He didn't tell me that he had already done so."

"When I called Brian, my bio father," said Lynette, "he started crying and saying how much he had loved my mother. And then I started crying, and we decided we should all get together in one place and pick up the pieces."

Missy added, her eyes glistening, "Brian told me about the note and how Sandra had waited for me to show up, but my parents had shuffled me off to my aunt's home in Spokane as soon as I told them about being pregnant. They were, still are, staunch Catholics and couldn't abide the shame they felt with me in the house."

"Is that why you gave up your daughter for adoption instead of raising her as a single parent?"

Missy nodded. "That, and the fact that being a single parent wasn't very common forty years ago. I wanted my daughter to have the best possible life with two parents." She dabbed her eyes and nose again. "I'm thrilled to be reunited with her."

Lynette hugged her mom and kissed her on the cheek. "I've always felt there was a piece of me missing. I knew I had been adopted and I was very much loved, but when I walked into your shop a couple of weeks ago and saw that desk, I knew I wanted it. I like vintage pieces, and it was very well preserved. I had no idea it held a clue that would lead you to my mother and father."

"I wondered why you didn't come back to get it like you said you would," said Christie.

"I'll have to blame an issue at work," said Lynette. "One of my senior caseworkers took emergency leave because of a death in the family so I had to cover her cases for a few days. And I didn't think to call you to explain. I'm so sorry."

"That's okay. I understand how those things happen. So, I remember your mentioning that your grandmother had one similar to it," said Christie, "but did you know your biological family at all?"

"No, although I was raised in a Catholic family in Spokane and at one point, Father Timothy, whom I know now is my uncle, was the priest at our parish. He used to look at me kinda funny but never said anything. He likely didn't know I was his sister's daughter, but maybe he suspected."

"You do have a strong resemblance," said Christie, laughing. "Brian told me about Sandra and leaving the note with her, so I came here to see if she was still working. Turns out her niece bought the business from her. Sandra didn't remember who she gave the note to at first, but she called a few days later and told me it was Jack Smith who promised to give it to you. He'd told her he knew you."

Missy grimaced. "Ugh. He hinted that I should go out with him even though he knew I was seeing Brian. He was kinda different, and I never felt comfortable around him." She shivered.

"I don't think he ever planned to give it to you, or maybe he never saw you again because you had already left town. Anyway, I found the note taped to the bottom of one of the drawers of the desk. And I wondered who 'Missy' and 'B' were. And who put the note there in the first place."

"Do you think it was Jack Smith?" asked Missy. "But how and when?"

"That's the part I still don't know," said Christie, "but, now that I have identified you as Missy and Brian as B, most of the mystery of the note is solved."

"Is Jack Smith still alive?" Missy rubbed her arms as if she were cold.

"Yes. He lives in the same house where his parents lived until they died. You might not have known that his father was the deputy sheriff during the time you were student teaching here in White Castle."

FIFTY

Christie entered her house to find Stormy perched on the back of the sofa, her big yellow eyes focused on the door. She scooped her up and asked, "Are you trying to tell me something, Stormy?" Christie fed the cat one of her favorite flavors — tuna — and poured herself a glass of cabernet.

She popped a CD of Chopin études into her Crosley player and curled up in her armchair. The familiar music flowed through the air as she ran through the day's events in her mind. She smiled as she thought about her role in reuniting Brian, Missy and Lynette. Then she shivered involuntarily when she recalled the latest call from Mr. Raspy Voice. She asked Stormy, now purring on her lap, "How could he order flowers if he was the man taken into custody? Maybe the man I followed, the man Conway took into custody, wasn't the flower buyer after all." Christie sighed. There still appeared to be an unsolved mystery.

She was listening to Étude Number Three, "Tristesse," when she heard a knock on the front door, breaking her reverie. She uprooted Stormy from her lap and turned down the music volume. She peeked through the peephole. Conway. After unlocking the door and inviting him in, she asked, "Are you going to tell me who you took into custody yesterday, since it obviously wasn't Mr. Raspy Voice after all?"

Conway grinned and took off his hat. "Let me have a little of whatever you're drinking, and I'll tell you the whole story." He added, "I'm off duty now, if you're wondering."

Stormy weaseled her way onto Conway's lap, where he sat on the sofa. Christie reclaimed her armchair after pouring a glass of wine for her visitor.

"I'm ready. So, who is the man who's been calling for the flowers? And who is Mr. Jones?"

Conway stroked Stormy's fur. "Let me start with the pool cue murder. When you found the note in the desk, you accidentally started a chain of events that had been lying dormant for forty years."

"You're blaming *me* for all this?" Christie asked with narrowed eyes.

He chuckled. "No, of course not. But when you were curious enough to start asking questions about the note and started piecing together some of the facts, you inadvertently caused some worry. Two of the players at that bar fight thought they'd never be caught for their part in it."

"Who?"

"I'll get to that. I know you talked to Bronco Carver, who had been convicted of the murder but maintained his innocence. I believed him when I talked with him, and I understand you did, too. So, someone else had to have been the person who wielded the fatal blow. I wondered who and why, so I started doing some investigation myself, with the help of your friend Jason Princeton and the old records that he had from the original proceedings."

"I thought you were blowing me off," said Christie.

"I was trying to keep you out of danger, actually. Because now, we jump to the present-day deaths of those receiving your flowers. Once I determined the owner of the SUV, who picked the bouquets up, I did some research and found out he had been a friend of someone from that case going back those forty years and had done some time for drug dealing along the way. He was willing to work out a deal and lay a trap, having been an accessory."

"Accessory to what?"

"Your so-called Mr. Jones was a friend of Arnold Youngman's younger brother Sam. Sam had had a relationship with the murderer, and Arnold was threatening to tell the other guy's father about it. Being gay wasn't socially acceptable in this community at the time. So the murderer took advantage of the bar fight that night — that Jones started, by the way — to kill Arnold Youngman. Jones's friend, Sam, kept quiet about the murder all these years because the two men had something on each other, and neither one wanted to let that information be known."

"You're killing me, Conway. Who's the other man?"

"Don't you want to know how your flowers were used to kill their targets?"

"Yes, and then will you tell me who the murderer was?"

Conway smiled. He seemed to be enjoying making Christie wait, much to her chagrin. "Your flowers weren't really deadly, as you know. Mr. Jones was the middleman. Once he picked up the flowers, he slipped some powdered fentanyl into the card envelope before delivering them to the recipient identified by Jack Smith. When the recipient opened the envelope, he likely inhaled enough to sicken, if not kill him. It only takes two milligrams to be lethal, by the way. Then, the victim would die a 'natural' death. And no one was the wiser. It wasn't until you followed Mr. Jones toward Easton and we apprehended the driver of the pickup that we figured that out. You said you saw an envelope exchange hands when the flowers were transferred from one vehicle to the other. It contained small packets of powdered fentanyl that had been provided by Sam. Remember, he had been convicted in the past for dealing drugs."

"That makes sense," said Christie. "I couldn't figure out how someone could die just from a bouquet of flowers with no real magical powers."

"It was too late, of course, to test the blood of the two men who died earlier, but I called the hospital. Remember that the third gentleman, the one at the nursing home, had been admitted. The lab tested his blood and found the fentanyl.

"Once in custody, and with the possibility of charges for attempted murder, we were able to persuade our suspect to lay a trap for Sam, and that's why there was one last call from Mr. Raspy Voice, as you called him. Mr. Jones told Sam he wasn't able to do the delivery that time, so Sam did it himself."

"So that's why he seemed to look a little different. I thought he was shorter but decided it was my imagination."

"Exactly. So, when he delivered the flowers to the house that Jack specified, he was arrested by the officers waiting inside."

Christie's mouth dropped open. "It was Jack Smith all along behind this? I don't understand."

FIFTY-ONE

Christie, Jason and Anita sat around the table at JoJo's on Saturday afternoon. Tall vanilla lattés accompanied by fresh maple bars, courtesy of Sandra, who had baked them that morning, were perfect for the cool, blustery weather. Christie related Conway's explanation of what really happened that night so long ago at the bar.

"So it was Jack Smith after all," said Anita. "I would never have guessed that it was him, being the deputy sheriff's son and all." She shook her head. "These maple bars are fantastic! Yum."

"But in a way, it makes sense," said Jason. "Nobody suspected him for that very reason. His father certainly wouldn't have fathomed his son being guilty of doing anything wrong, especially murder. Or if he did, he looked the other way. And he already had evidence pointing to someone else."

"Right," said Christie. "In those days, being gay was still behind doors, so Jack must have felt threatened when Arnold, Sam Youngman's older brother, threatened to tell the deputy sheriff, or maybe the mom, that their son was gay. That was what the fight was really about, not over Missy. So when Arnold collapsed and Jack heard the sirens, he had to get out. He probably thrust the cue stick into the hands of the first person he saw, who happened to be Bronco Carver, a truly innocent bystander."

"Do you know what triggered the recent spate of murders?" Anita asked. "Probably no one else around even thought about that old murder from forty years ago."

"Unfortunately," said Christie, "it may well have been me, when I asked Jack about the note I found in the desk. My aunt had suggested I ask him about that old murder because he would have been about the same age as the other young guys at the bar. And had lived around here all his life."

"You can't blame yourself," said Jason, placing a hand on Christie's arm. "How could you have known?"

"He could certainly have worried that Christie would get too nosy and maybe even figure it out. It's like she opened a Pandora's box." Anita reached for a second maple bar.

"As it turns out," said Christie. "that desk had been in his parents' home. When Jack took the note from Sandra, he taped it under one of the drawers, possibly in a hurry, not ever expecting it to see the light of day, and probably forgot all about it. He panicked, I guess, when he realized the desk and note were in my store. And he wanted to get the note back, which is why he had one of his friends steal the desk. Of course, I had already removed the note and given it to Jason for safekeeping, so he didn't find it."

"Didn't you say that you didn't know where the desk came from?" asked Anita.

"Yes, although I found a note in my grandmother's files that seemed to refer to the desk. I now realize it must have been donated by Jack's mother before she died. It had been in her attic for years, and I'm sure Jack didn't know it had found its way to my grandma's shop until I told him about the note."

Jason signaled for three more lattés, then asked, "How did Mr. Jones and Sam Youngman get involved? I always wonder why people don't understand that when more than two people get involved in doing something, especially murder, there's more opportunity for things to go wrong."

Christie finished her maple bar and took a second one. "I adore these!" She licked a finger. "Chief Conway told me that Sam, the younger brother, was Jack's gay partner and was also culpable in the original murder by the fact that he didn't come forward. When the note reappeared, he and Jack concocted a plan to get rid of the remaining witnesses from the bar fight to make it difficult or impossible to ever be implicated should the whole deal come to light. He talked a friend of his — our 'Mr. Jones' — into doing the flower deliveries."

Anita asked, "Would Brian have also been culpable because he ran away at the time?"

"I asked Conway that very question. He said 'Probably not' because he was innocent of any actual wrong-doing. Apparently Brian called and tried to offer testimony but it wasn't considered strong enough against the deputy sheriff's account of witnessing Bronco with the cue stick."

Jason asked, "Did Conway ever reveal who he took into custody the day you were tailing the SUV and Ford F-150? I understand you didn't know who it was at the time. Right?"

"Right, and yes, he told me that the state troopers arrested both Mr. Jones — his real last name, by the way — and Jack Smith. They were able to get cooperation from the two of them to trap Sam as well. As I said, Sam had provided the fentanyl that Mr. Jones added to the envelopes before he delivered the flowers. Anyway, Jack made that last phone call to my shop and asked Sam to do the delivery because Mr. Jones was unavailable. He was arrested when he stepped inside the house. Conway said he cussed a blue streak."

Jason chuckled. "I'll bet he did!"

Anita raised her hand as if in a classroom. "Another question. Does Jack have a raspy voice all the time? I've never heard him talk."

Christie shook her head. "I've talked with him, and he sounds normal, but he was using some kind of voice changer over the phone to make him sound very hoarse. Conway said he found it at the house when they searched. He also found the list of names Jack and Sam planned to murder. Brian and Bronco were at the top."

Anita gasped. "Good thing you were tailing him and got Conway involved."

Jason drained his latté. "You haven't told us how Jack actually killed his victims. I know your flowers aren't deadly, but obviously something was."

"Conway told me that Fentanyl is so strong that simply inhaling a couple of milligrams of the powder can be enough to kill someone, or at least make them very ill. Especially if they're older and already have heart disease, like Mr. Ferguson did."

"Pretty clever but so devious," said Jason.

"Have you talked with Missy or Brian since this all transpired?" asked Anita. "Do you think they're going to see each other?"

Christie grinned broadly. "Missy told me they're planning a vacation together — Missy, Brian, Lynette and Lynette's fiancé, who was driving the red Porsche that day. They'll be able to spend a lot of time getting to know each other."

Anita sighed dramatically, "I just love happy endings!"

Jason said, "You might have to hang another sign at your shop that says 'Amateur Sleuth — Inquire Within.'"

Christie groaned. "I don't think so. I'll stick to flowers, thank you."

The End

AUTHOR'S NOTES

Writing *Killer Flowers* was a lot of fun!

The idea of writing true cozy mysteries has been floating around in my head for a while. My other series with Julia Fairchild as my protagonist technically fits the "cozy" category (no sex, no graphic violence) but Julia stumbles onto her mysteries while she's on vacation, for the most part, whereas cozy mysteries typically occur within one's own town.

Christie O'Mara, as the new owner of *Christie's Flower Shoppe*, will have the mysteries fall into her lap, or more precisely, out of her flowers.

Creating new characters is a bit like choosing your playmates. A couple of characters are based on a composite of real people, such as Aunt Doris and Jason. Others are completely made up out of my imagination. Christie, for example, might be the kind of bubbly cheerleader-person that I wanted to be as a teen. Anita represents my image of sophistication plopped into a small town.

I hope you enjoy this first book in the series. I can hardly wait to find out what Christie does in her next book!

Thank you for reading!
PJ Peterson
www.pjpetersonauthor.com

ACKNOWLEDGMENTS

Writing a novel is a labor of love, much of the time. It also requires a lot of steps for the story to become a novel that can actually be published!

First, I thank my lovely Developmental Editor, Sandra Herner, whom I "met" via Reedsy. I think she knows my characters better than I do! She offers excellent feedback with helpful suggestions to resolve the tangled messes I tend to create when my brain is going faster than my fingers.

Secondly, thanks go to my friend Angela Thompson. She listens to me as I talk through potential scenarios and offers thoughtful insight. And hasn't fired me yet!

Third, my über-talented copy editor, Kathleen Costello (kcostello@grammartogo.com), not only corrects my not-quite-perfect punctuation and grammar, but catches inconsistencies that I hadn't noticed and offers solutions. Thank you!

Of course, I must thank my friends and readers, beta and otherwise.

I would love to hear from you!

PJ Peterson

pj@pjpetersonauthor.com